Civic Plan # 19/8/04

WE'LL MEET AGAIN

Recent Titles by Rosemary Anne Sisson from Severn House Large Print

FIRST LOVE, LAST LOVE
FOOTSTEP ON THE STAIR

WE'LL MEET AGAIN

Rosemary Anne Sisson

Severn House Large Print
London & New York

This first large print edition published in Great Britain 2004 by
SEVERN HOUSE LARGE PRINT BOOKS LTD of
9-15 High Street, Sutton, Surrey, SM1 1DF.
Regular print edition published 2003 by
Severn House Publishers, London and New York.
This first large print edition published in the USA 2004 by
SEVERN HOUSE PUBLISHERS INC., of
595 Madison Avenue, New York, NY 10022.

British Library Cataloguing in Publication Data

Sisson, Rosemary Anne, 1923 -
    We'll meet again. - Large print ed.
    1. Great Britain. Royal Air Force - Fiction
    2. World War, 1939 – 1945 - Fiction
    3. Love stories
    4. Large type books
    I. Title
    II. Sisson, Rosemary Anne, 1923 -. Finders Keepers
    823.9'14 [F]

    ISBN 0-7278-7371-7

Printed and bound in Great Britain by
MPG Books Ltd, Bodmin, Cornwall.

To my Mother,
the shabash-wallah,
with love.

Author's Introduction

It was my sister who told me the story of an old college friend who was in the A.T.S. (the women's branch of the Army) and who fell in love with a fellow officer. But he was married, and she was a vicar's daughter; so, for her at least, a love-affair was out of the question. They agreed to part and, because their feelings for each other were so strong, they promised that they wouldn't even keep in touch. Then, after the war, his wife died, and he didn't know where to find my sister's friend.

Because my war service was spent plotting aircraft, I changed the setting to the R.A.F. and, since I never met my sister's friend, I had to invent the characters. But I'll always be grateful to my sister – and to that A.T.S. officer – who, all unknowing, gave me the story of her life and love.

One

'Sandy's promotion has come through,' said Tom.

It was a little time before Anne answered, as though the words were coming from a long way off and it took a while for her to hear them and find the right reply.

'Oh, good. He must be pleased.'

'Well,' said Tom, 'he says he'll be glad of the extra money.'

'What does his wife say?' inquired Anne.

'She doesn't care about the money. She wanted the extra stripe to show off in the anteroom.'

Anne heard the smile in his voice and felt her face smile, too. She wondered if his smile was as unconvincing as hers. She did not dare look at him directly.

'She's entitled to her simple pleasures.'

'You think so?' inquired Tom. 'She won't be satisfied until poor old Sandy's got scrambled egg on his cap!'

They both laughed at that, and then there

9

was a great roar of laughter from the bar. They looked toward it and saw a young man in RAF uniform, with wings on his breast, doing a handstand among the empty glasses, urged on with hilarity by those around him.

'What on earth is Jimmy Pratt doing?' asked Anne.

'I imagine,' said Tom, 'that he is demonstrating how he got his feet caught in his parachute when he bailed out.'

They looked at each other then, and their eyes met and held. A voice broke in.

'Hello, Tom. I hear your posting's come through.'

It was Bender – dear old Squadron Leader Bender, with his well-worn wings that dated from the Royal Flying Corps and his days in Iraq. Tom and Anne looked toward him as he made his way through the crowded little pub.

'That's right,' Tom called back. 'I'm off today.'

Bender arrived beside them, his round, ruddy cheeks glowing.

'Sorry to lose you, old fellow.'

'Thanks,' said Tom.

'How's Betty?' inquired Bender.

Anne took a sip of her drink.

'She's fine, thanks,' Tom replied.

'Still down in Dorset with the children?'

'That's right,' said Tom. 'They're staying with my parents.'

'Good idea,' said Bender. 'Hopeless, dragging the kids all around the countryside. Much better let 'em settle down, make a home. I bet they like Dorset.'

'They seem to,' said Tom, but his lips were stiff. 'Lucy's taken up riding. She fell off the pony three times the first day.'

'Good God!' said Bender.

'She said she never enjoyed herself so much in her whole life,' said Tom, 'and she's only four.'

'Jolly good!' said Bender with enthusiasm. He laughed, and Anne and Tom laughed with him.

Their laughter was echoed from the bar, where young Jimmy Pratt was drinking the three half-pints that his handstand had won him. Bender looked toward him.

'Young idiot!' he said tolerantly. 'Well, must get a quick snifter.'

He turned toward the crowd at the bar but paused.

'Anne, you coming to the dance tonight?' he asked.

It was Anne's turn to smile, stiff-lipped.

'Oh, I can't, sir, unfortunately. I'm on duty.'

11

'Too bad,' said Bender. 'Well, cheerio, Tom. All the best.'

'Good-bye,' said Tom.

Bender continued toward the bar and the cheerful, noisy group round Jimmy.

Anne and Tom sat motionless, the invisible clasp of their hands under the table known only to themselves.

'It can't be right,' said Anne, 'for anyone to suffer like this. Can it?'

'I don't know,' said Tom.

They were silent for a moment, and then Anne said, 'Isn't it awful? You find yourself talking in clichés. In a minute we'll be saying, "This thing is bigger than both of us!"'

He turned his head to smile at her, and this time the smile was real, part of their quick, loving understanding of each other's thoughts.

'I remember once at school,' said Anne, 'I fainted in prayers. And when I came to, do you know what I said?'

Tom was still looking at her, smiling. He shook his head.

'I said, "Where am I?" I really did.'

She tried to laugh and found her eyes full of tears.

'Oh, God!' said Tom.

They sat motionless in their own private

agony, made all the sharper by the noise and hilarity about them. Cheerful voices came from a group of fighter pilots nearby who were leaning against the dark upright posts that propped up the low smoke-stained ceiling. These were the young men whose progress across the skies Anne's WAAFs plotted every day and every night, pushing little bars across the map table with miniature shovels, like a travesty of croupiers recording wins and losses in roulette.

'So I thought,' said one young flying officer with stripes, 'I thought, "That's funny; those are supposed to be *our* guns. Why are they firing at *me*?"'

'You were over France,' suggested his neighbour.

'Certainly not,' replied the flying officer, with dignity. 'Coming in over the coast, I was, as good as gold. But then I heard a little voice in my ear.'

'It said "Your navigation stinks, old boy."'

'No, it didn't.'

He took a hearty gulp of beer.

'Come on, Freddy,' demanded another of his companions. 'What did your little voice say?'

'There was only one voice,' replied Freddy, 'and it said "you bloody fool, look behind you!" So I looked behind me, and

13

there was this doodlebug chuntering along, right on me tail. I peeled off so fast, I left me markings behind!'

They all roared with laughter.

Anne thought, 'They're laughing because he nearly died.'

It was as though the moment war broke out in 1939, everyone decided that the only way to get through it was to laugh at danger, and they'd been laughing ever since – at Hitler and the Siegfried Line, at Goering and his medals, at Dunkirk and the British Expeditionary Force (Back Every Fortnight), even at the bombing that tore into their last security, their homes, leaving only peeling wallpaper and broken gas pipes behind. And now, five years later, these pilots were still laughing, as they had always laughed – aloud, that is – at death. But the harsh lesson of war was that death was the least of its terrors. Not death but parting was the deepest anguish.

'You know something ridiculous?' said Anne. 'I don't even remember the first time I saw you.'

'I remember the first time I saw *you*,' said Tom. 'You were leaning over the table to check an SOS plot, and I thought, "Gosh, that WAAF officer's got a beautiful pair of legs!"'

14

He looked at her.

'You're blushing.'

'I'm not!' said Anne indignantly, but she knew she was.

Anne had always thought that men and women fell in love because of a meeting of minds and hearts – perhaps even of souls. That was how it was portrayed by all the authorities upon whom she had hitherto relied – Charlotte and Emily Brontë, Louisa May Alcott, her father. She was astonished to find, even as she blushed, even at this moment, that she was delighted to know that the first thing Tom had noticed about her was her legs. But she wasn't going to admit it, even to Tom.

'It was the station dance, wasn't it?' she said. 'That was when it all began.'

Two

Anne remembered Tom standing in front of her, his expression formal and polite.

'May I?'

It was always a relief to be asked to dance. Most of the unmarried pilots were younger than Anne and only wanted to have a fling with the local talent. Of the rest, the wives now mostly lived on the station. Anne was quite accustomed to standing and talking to them, secretly tapping her feet in time to the music, knowing that they knew intuitively that she would never try to steal their husbands.

'May I?' said Tom.

Anne laughed ruefully as she took his hands.

'I'm a hopeless dancer,' she said.

'I'm sure you're not,' said Tom, and drew her close.

Tom was a beautiful dancer. Her body moved with his body, and her feet instinctively followed his. Maybe that should have given some warning of danger, but it didn't because Tom was telling her about his wife, Betty, and how they had won dancing contests together at Streatham Ballroom, where they met.

'Good heavens!' exclaimed Tom suddenly.

'What is it?'

'Didn't Bender say his wife was coming this weekend?'

'Ye-es? Good heavens!'

As Tom swung her around in his arms, Anne saw Squadron Leader Bender in the doorway and, beside him, a large lady with glossy black hair, who wore a mauve crepe dress decorated with purple sequins.

'You don't think...?' said Anne, awed.

Bender had always been so awfully posh. The rest of them had scrambled into the RAF one way or the other because of the war, rather like temporary gents in the trenches of the First World War. But Bender, with his RFC wings and his occasional 'By Jove!' brought with him a whiff of *Dawn Patrol*, of highly polished boots and Sam Browne belt, and of a Royal Air Force that was socially acceptable, a sort of flying Brigade of Guards. Somehow if they had pictured his wife at all, it would have been as extremely ladylike and rather boring, the sort of woman who talked about her garden

17

and wore a drooping black dress adorned only by an antique brooch.

'Perhaps his wife couldn't come,' said Tom, 'so he brought a local barmaid. He does have a bit of an eye for the girls. Remember that little redhead he brought last time?'

The music came to an end, and Tom's final twirl brought them to a halt alongside. Bender beamed.

'Ah, Tom, Anne,' he said, 'I want you to meet my wife.'

Up close, Mavis Bender was even more astonishing. It was hard to believe that her makeup was intentional, but since it had clearly taken a great deal of hard work, it must have been. The base seemed to be white enamel, and on each cheek was a symmetrical pink blob of singular brightness with only a slight fading into a lighter pink around it. Her eyebrows had been completely plucked and replaced by twin arches whose light brown color was at variance with the glossy black of her hair. As for her mascara, it was so thick that it hung in blobs, and behind these beaded black curtains lurked a pair of surprisingly green eyes.

Tom was still holding Anne's hand as the dance came to an end, and she felt him give

18

it a secret, ecstatic squeeze. She spoke hastily.

'I hope you had a good journey, Mrs Bender?'

'*A good journey?*' said Mavis Bender. 'Listen, I had to change three times. I had to stand in the corridor all the way to London, and the soldiers were all drunk – I'll tell you that for nothing – and then, after I had to wait forty minutes for a taxi across London, I got to Chichester, and I found there wasn't a train for another hour. An hour!'

'I say,' said Tom, 'bad luck!'

The music started again. Tom gave Anne's hand a final squeeze before releasing it.

'Er – would you care to dance?' he inquired.

'Oh, my poor feet!' said Mavis Bender. 'Well, all right. If you insist!'

Partly because of this first encounter and partly because the other officers and their wives tended to back nervously away, Anne and Tom found themselves spending most of the evening with Bender and his wife, in a slightly eccentric foursome. Mavis really was quite good company, and there was no doubt that Bender was immensely proud of her. Unfortunately, however, as she downed more whiskies and reflected upon the discomforts of her journey, it occurred to her

19

that Bender could have saved her the final exasperating hour's wait if he had met her at Chichester. In vain Bender told her that he had been on duty and assured her that in any event, he was saving the gasoline to take her out.

'Oh, yays?' said Mavis, her voice rising in alcoholic indignation, the splendid Birmingham vowels breaking through to stunning effect, 'you was going to take me out, was yer? And when might that be, might I ask? Next week, I suppose, after I'd gone. Why couldn't you get orff your arse and meet me at Chichester?'

Tom's hand gripped Anne's elbow. The mirth they shared ran through them like an electric current. They retired, side by side and in step, to the far end of the bar.

'She's only here for the weekend,' murmured Anne, 'and she's come all this way and had that terrible journey. Are they going to quarrel all the time?'

'Odd,' said Tom. 'Very odd.'

Anne saw his humorously solemn round face and the gleam in his gray-green eyes, and she should have known then, but she didn't. She never thought that a delicious shared amusement in dear old Bender and his gloriously inappropriate wife could be dangerous.

'Now is the time,' sang the leader of the band, with his corporal's stripe and his Brylcreem hair, 'for us to say good night.'

Anne was clasped tightly in Tom's arms; she could feel the outline of his cigarette case pressing into her breast, but they were talking about Betty and the children and about her father and the rectory in Norfolk, and there was no danger. No danger at all.

Anne had sometimes wondered what her life would have been like if she had joined up, as most of her contemporaries did, as soon as the war broke out. Presumably she would have met young RAF officers of her own age, married one of them, perhaps, and by now be a war widow with one or two children. She might even be into her second marriage because pilots' wives did seem to marry again, forming a sort of respectable *cadre* of matrimonial camp followers, an emotional inheritance from one fighter pilot to another, some marrying as many as three in succession. But Anne's mother had been taken ill early in 1939, and she, as sole daughter of the house, stayed behind to nurse her.

It had not seemed at all heroic to stay on in that Norfolk rectory not far from Nelson's home, while other people put on uniforms, drilled and trained and fought.

21

Dunkirk happened and the Battle of Britain, and Anne helped the little maid, Gladys, to wash and iron her father's surplices.

'Oh, *good*, darling!' exclaimed her mother, when Anne displayed them. 'Clergymen in grubby surplices do look somehow ... so *silly*!'

As the bombs fell on London, Anne often struggled out of bed after a troubled night to go to the early communion service because the communicants were now so few that her father became depressed.

'Oh, *thank* you, darling,' her mother would say as she hurried in afterward with the breakfast tray and medicines. 'You know, it's like free tickets in the theatre – it swells the numbers.'

Every week, Anne bicycled into Thorpe to get their rations and, after Gladys left with an air of ineffable patriotism to join the NAAFI and find a soldier-husband, Anne took on the cooking. She also found herself saddled with 'doing the flowers' in the church, the local ladies being now too busy working for the WVS and organizing canteens.

'Thank heaven!' whispered her mother, her skin like papyrus and her eyes gleaming like bright candles. 'At least Mrs Fancourt's delphiniums won't be standing at attention all around the pulpit!'

But behind it all was the anguish of the fluctuating improvement and deterioration of her mother's health and the long, dragging strain of pretending that there was hope even when all hope was gone. On the night before her mother died, Anne woke in the armchair to see those bright hazel eyes fixed on her face. She started up.

'Mummy! Did you want...?'

The dark head moved infinitesimally. Anne had to slide to her knees, leaning close to hear.

'Don't stay here after I'm dead.'

Anne took a breath to protest, but the gleam of amusement in the hazel eyes prevented her.

'Darling, did you think I didn't know?'

They smiled at each other, and Anne felt a great burden roll off her heart. It was as though until that moment the entire weight of her mother's death had been hers, but now they shared it.

'Don't stay here,' said her mother.

'But, Daddy...'

The neat head moved again, a tiny but minatory movement. The miserly breath measured the words out, syllable by syllable.

'It was all right for me. He ... always ...

23

made me laugh. But ... you ... mustn't ... mustn't...'

There was a moment when, with the pain and the painkillers, everything was slipping away from her, but she fought back.

'You must make your own life.'

There was a long silence, and then, like the last breath that flutters the flame, 'Darling! Thank you!'

'Mummy!' cried Anne. 'Oh, Mummy!'

Thank you for what? What had she done? What *could* she do, when nothing would hold back pain or prevent that last slow, muddy walk into the churchyard, with her father seeming even more helpless by reason of the crisp white surplice that was somehow supposed to shield him from all normal feelings, even grief, but didn't?

But later, Anne understood that hidden debt that her mother, with almost her last breath, had acknowledged. She found that when her deferred call up papers came and she joined the WAAFs, she had already and irretrievably yielded to her dying mother, to her grieving father, an insouciance and resilience that would never come again. It was a gift freely, if unknowingly, given, and yet ... it was the gift of her youth.

She rose swiftly through the ranks. As a parson's daughter, she was instantly recog-

24

nized as being 'officer material' and, accustomed to responsibility, she accepted the offer of a commission. Her WAAFs brought to her their foolish love affairs, and she gave them good, sound advice, as though she herself was quite unlikely ever to find herself in such a maelstrom of emotions. The officers' wives, knowing that she was virtuous and unpredatory, confided in her as though she was their mother instead of an unattached girl of twenty-two. She posed no threat. Her blue eyes were friendly, not acquisitive. Her brown hair shone with golden lights, but they were natural and not enhanced by peroxide. Altogether a nice girl, they would think, and so easy to talk to. As for the officers, they all said she was a good sort and bought her gin and limes and treated her as a friend. That is, until the station dance, when Tom said, 'May I?' and they danced together, and he made her laugh.

It was during that first evening that Anne and Tom discovered they both enjoyed the cinema.

'Betty and I used to go three times a week,' said Tom, 'but it's not much fun going by yourself.'

'No,' said Anne with feeling. 'It isn't.'

'Do you fancy Bing Crosby in *Going My*

Way?' asked Tom.

The film was an immensely sentimental story about an old Roman Catholic priest who was really over the hill and the new, eager young priest, Bing Crosby, who had been sent to replace him but was too polite to say so. When Barry Fitzgerald's old Irish mother tottered in to the old Irish tune of 'Toora-loora-loora,' Anne and Tom turned to each other and grinned ruefully at the discovery that both had tears running down their cheeks.

They went out to dinner afterward at a little restaurant recommended by Squadron Leader Bender.

'Horse,' said Tom, taking his first bite of the tough, sweet-tasting steak. 'Definitely horse.'

'Not at all,' said Anne firmly. 'They're just clever with their rations.'

'I love an innocent and trusting nature,' said Tom.

'Isn't it odd,' remarked Anne, as they chewed their way through the steak with hungry determination, 'that whenever Hollywood has a religious scene, it's always Roman Catholic? I suppose they're more pictorial – all that lighting of candles and crossing oneself and so on.'

'I've never thought about it,' said Tom,

26

'but I suppose it's true. One religion is much like another to me.'

Anne looked at him, stunned. It emerged that he and Betty had been married in the Church of England because she and her mother wanted it, but that he really didn't think it was important.

'Not *important*?' exclaimed Anne. 'If you're making vows to love each other till death do you part, surely it should mean something?'

'Of course it does,' said Tom. 'But as long as you mean the vows, what does it matter where you make them?'

The argument lasted until they got back to the station.

'I tell you what,' said Tom, as he opened the car door for her outside the WAAF officer quarters, 'let's go to that musical next week. Betty Hutton. I love Betty Hutton. Nothing to argue about with Betty Hutton.'

'I hate Betty Hutton!' said Anne, and they began to laugh and clutched each other.

'Sh-sh,' said Anne, conscious of the sentry on the gate and the dark windows above them. But she was still laughing as she walked along the green-painted corridor to her room.

During the following weeks, Anne was

27

constantly aware of Tom. As soon as she came on duty, she glanced to see if he was there and, if he wasn't, she watched for him and knew the moment he arrived.

'Ma'am! Ma'am!' the WAAFs would call, 'can I go to lunch now?' or 'Ma'am, should this "Hostile" plot still be here?' And Anne would respond, exactly as she always had, but it was though she lived all the time a second, secret life, of which Tom, day by day, was becoming more and more the centre.

Of course she knew she was falling in love. She would have had to be an idiot not to know. But it was a very special kind of love that she knew from the beginning could have no future because Tom was married. When he casually put his arm around her as they left the movies or took her elbow at the bar or smiled into her eyes as they danced, she knew that she was no more to him than a slight romantic substitute for his wife. She was glad for his sake and for Betty's that she could in this way bridge the gap of their parting without endangering their marriage, and if in the end she herself suffered a little, it would be worth it. Apart from anything else, she had never really been in love before and delighted in the novelty of it; also, perhaps, she felt some relief to know that

28

she was not, as she had sometimes thought, love-proof. He would never know how she felt about him, and it would all be over when one or the other of them was posted or when the war came to an end – if it ever did. Meanwhile she was content to enjoy the subtle sensation of being in love and the secret pleasure she took in every moment she was with him.

It was ironic that Tom and Anne met in 1944, which was such a miserable year as far as the war was concerned. They had all been depressed by the renewal of the bombing of London and by the sense of useless struggle, like a tug-of-war in which first one side had the advantage and then the other, but neither could ever win.

'I sometimes think,' said Anne, after a particularly bad night when a Mosquito Night Fighter had hit an elm tree on its way home and crashed, killing both the crew, 'that we'll never live an ordinary life again. It sounds like a silly thing to moan about when men are getting killed, but I hate to think I went through the whole of last year and never heard a cuckoo – and I'll probably do the same thing this year.'

'No, you won't,' said Tom. 'That's one thing we *can* take care of. Let's take a picnic up on the downs tomorrow.'

'We *can't*!' said Anne. And then, *'Can* we?'

Funnily enough, it wasn't easy. In wartime, even a picnic had to be idented for, or wheedled out of the kitchens, and when they drove to the woods, Tom had to bluff his way past the sentry because of the nearby radar station.

'It's ridiculous,' said Anne as they drove on. 'Who on earth decided to put a sentry on woods full of nothing but primroses?'

'Hitler,' answered Tom, and suddenly they were both laughing.

Anne had felt some awkwardness as the sentry eyed them cynically before waving them on, but now that vanished, and they were like two children playing truant who had been spotted by the headmaster and gotten clean away with it.

From that moment, it was a day stolen from time. War, which robs months and years of life, sometimes gives in return such days, to be remembered long after the other dark days are forgotten.

When the deeply rutted track gave out, they climbed the gate and walked on, carrying the picnic in the usual repository for anything except a gas mask – Anne's gas mask holder. Chaffinches twittered in the hedges and the grassy track was lined with cow's parsley. Then at last even the track

30

vanished, and they were upon the open downs. They felt a marvelous sense of liberation as they sat on the short, springy grass, with a skylark singing invisibly high above their heads and early butterflies fluttering above the clover. Even the lunch of doorstep-thick Spam sandwiches had something of the quality of the nursery – spartan but comforting. There was a thermos of tea and a can of condensed milk, and it was while Anne was throwing the dregs from the tin mugs onto the wild thyme that they heard a cuckoo calling from the wood below.

'Oh, listen!' she cried.

The cuckoo's voice was like a sign from heaven, a pure rainbow of sound, giving assurance that the war would not go on forever and that the dreadful awareness of tyranny and torture, fear and suffering, would be lifted at last.

'Oh, Tom!' she said, turning to him a face full of joy. 'He's still there. At least the cuckoo's still there!'

She put her hand on his arm, and Tom, smiling, put his hand on hers and then, still keeping her hand in his, tucked it under his arm, and they lay side by side, innocent as children, listening to the invisible fluting of the lark high above and the bell-like song of

31

the cuckoo far below.

It was hard to turn back to reality, but a cloud came over the sun, and the lark dropped down to its nest, and the cuckoo's voice wandered, grew fainter, and was silent. Anne and Tom smiled at each other ruefully as they loosened their hands and began to get up. The walk back to the car, although it was downhill, seemed much farther than the way up.

'I know,' said Anne. 'We must take something back. Let's pick some primroses.'

'Put them in a jam jar in the middle of the plotting table,' suggested Tom.

'Good idea. If we can find a jam jar!'

Her heavy, black laced-up shoes trudged amid the brambles and fallen leaves as she picked the slender stems, putting them delicately, one by one, into an exquisite sweet-scented bunch. She looked up and saw Tom watching her.

'Come on, lazy!' she said.

He smiled and shook his head.

'Men can't pick primroses,' he said. 'They're much too clumsy.'

Anne felt a subtle pleasure at his words. In spite of her black shoes and stockings and the mannish style of her grey uniform skirt and jacket, shirt, collar and tie, she was glad to know that he thought of her as a woman.

32

She went on stooping among the saplings, picking the soft green leaves and fragile flowers, but always she was aware of Tom, standing watching her and smiling. When her hands were full, she stepped out onto the muddy path and held the fragrant bunch to his nose.

'Isn't that beautiful?' she said.

'Beautiful!' he replied and pulled her into his arms and kissed her.

Anne had never been kissed on the lips before. She had been brought up to think that that only happened when two people were engaged – perhaps only after they were married. Her knowledge of the precise details of the sexual act was rather sketchy, but she was pretty sure that kissing on the lips was the preliminary to it and, rather to her surprise, she found that she didn't much like it. She fought free from Tom's grasp and stepped back, dropping most of the primroses.

'How *could* you!' she exclaimed.

'Darling!'

'Don't call me that!'

'But you know I love you,' said Tom.

'How *can* you?' said Anne. 'You're married!'

'Oh, for God's sake!' said Tom, 'you must have known I was falling in love with you.'

'Please don't swear,' said Anne, coldly.

That annoyed Tom as, subconsciously, she knew it would. But then he had annoyed her because what he said was true, and she didn't want to admit it.

'If you felt so strongly about my being married, why did you go out with me?' Tom demanded.

'Because I thought you knew how to behave.'

'I'm *sorry*!' said Tom in a tone that wasn't sorry at all but furious. 'I didn't realize you were just a stupid, priggish, little tease!'

There was a stunned pause before Anne spoke with outraged calm. 'We'd better get back,' she said and stooped and began to pick up the primroses.

Once she had begun, she bitterly regretted it. She felt like a perfect fool stooping there, picking up primroses one by one while Tom stood and watched her in a deadly silence, but an absurd obstinacy made her continue. Beastly primroses! How on earth many had she picked? There must be a hundred of them, the stems so fragile that they kept bending and breaking, her hands so clumsy with rage that she could hardly pick them up anyway. She straightened at last, and then saw that she had missed one. Tom bent and picked it up.

'Allow me,' he said and elaborately presented it to her.

'Thank you,' said Anne loftily and added it to the ragged and crushed bunch before turning toward the car.

They drove back to the station in the same deadly silence. Tom stopped the car outside her quarters, and she got out.

'I think the less we see of each other, the better,' said Tom.

'I quite agree,' said Anne.

She slammed the door, and Tom drove away. Anne threw the bunch of primroses in the nearest waste basket, and a week later she went on leave.

Three

Leave was supposed to be a sort of holiday camp where exhausted warriors had fun and renewed their strength. No one acknowledged that it just might involve instead a large and draughty rectory in Norfolk, skeleton meals, and a father plunged in gloom. Only her father, thought Anne, could turn a world war into a personal crisis

35

of faith. He had always believed that man was essentially good, only needing a little help from Christ to be perfect, and that everything in this world created by God was for the best, with the aid of a little prayer. He had managed to convince himself that he had triumphantly surmounted the sorrow of his wife's death, assisted by his Christian faith. But now ... if only, Anne thought, he would admit that his depression derived from the loss of that dear human companion whose laughter had illuminated his life of dedication. But, no, the wavering of his faith could not be attributed to such a small and natural cause. Anne, fearful for her own faith in a deeply personal dilemma, found no help in hearing her father preaching gloomy sermons in an empty and musty church about the problem of evil in a world where he had never really ventured.

On the last night of her leave, she made a supper of reconstituted scrambled eggs, and they sat together by the fire. It was colder than in Sussex, but at least they were never short of firewood.

'I'm afraid, my dear,' said her father, 'that this has not been a very cheerful leave for you.'

'It's not a very cheerful time for anyone,' answered Anne quietly.

36

Glancing up, she was surprised by the acuteness in the clear blue eyes fixed upon hers.

'But I fancy,' said her father, 'that all is not quite well with you personally just now.'

Anne found tears running down her cheeks.

'No,' she said. 'Not very well.'

Anyone but her father would have put a hand on hers or opened his arms for a comforting embrace, but instead the rector ate another forkful of reconstituted egg.

'I'm sure, my dear,' he said, 'that you will do what is right and that God will help you.'

The journey back from Norfolk was dreadful. Like most clergymen's children, Anne had been brought up to have a high tolerance of discomfort. Hard pews, cold bedrooms, constantly interrupted meals, and the kind of physical hard labour at church fetes and rummage sales that would make a coal miner demur had all combined to prepare her more than most of her middle-class contemporaries for the increasing rigors of wartime life. But she found now that her unhappiness, which should have deadened other senses, seemed to make her more susceptible to discomfort – or, rather, that the physical discomfort seemed to make her misery more unbearable.

She had left early in the morning to catch the slow train to Norwich. It was too dark to see out, and the windows were almost completely blacked over anyway. She had the compartment to herself, which was welcome at first, but then, as she sat huddled in the corner while the train jerked and lingered its way along the Norfolk villages, she began to feel as though she was in a coffin being trundled through a cemetery.

She had been involved in a silly, degrading little love affair – no, not even that – a commonplace episode in which she had behaved cheaply and been punished for it.

'Stupid, priggish, little tease!'

'I don't like that woman,' she remembered her mother remarking of the snobbish wife of one of the local dignitaries. 'She gives people the "come hither" look, and when they come, she kicks them on the shins.'

Anne had given the 'come hither' look to Tom, and the perfectly predictable result had ended their friendship. He would soon forget her or, perhaps, would just remember her as that silly WAAF officer who led him on and then kicked him on the shin. She would not so easily forget him. All she had done, in the end, was to sicken the memory of their time together.

At Norwich there was a long wait for the

38

London train. Crowds of cheerful Americans from the bomber stations surged about the platform and clogged the sole refreshment stand, shouting orders and flourishing dollar bills. Anne's father had urged her to bring sandwiches from home, but she refused, thinking he looked half-starved already, and saying she would get food on the journey. When at last the London train pulled into the station, she still hadn't managed to fight her way to the counter, and a final desperate foray as everyone else rushed out produced only an empty plate and the words, uttered with the familiar, if obscure, note of triumph: 'Sorry, m'dear. All gone.'

It was too late now to get a seat. Resigned at last to standing in a crowded corridor, Anne found herself next to an American, who smiled down at her appreciatively.

'Hi, there!' he said. 'A pretty little lady like you shouldn't be standing.'

He jerked his head toward the first-class compartment behind them.

'You want me to get one of those guys out of there?'

He was an airman and the 'guys' were officers, but, Anne supposed, he believed in the American version of democracy – every man as good as his neighbour, even in the armed forces.

'Please don't bother,' she said in the most English accent she could manage.

He shrugged.

'Suit yerself, ma'am,' he said and turned away.

Anne knew, guiltily, that the reason she had snubbed his kindness had nothing to do with a desire to maintain discipline but was entirely due to that unabashed look of admiration in his eyes. If she couldn't see that look in Tom's eyes, she didn't want to see it in anyone else's.

The train stopped outside Liverpool Street station for one of those wearisome, un-explained delays that now gave travel an extra nightmare quality. Anne, shifting from one aching foot to another, realized that she yet had to get across London and would probably miss her connecting train. The line for taxis was enormous, and the taxi drivers did their best to accept only American servicemen, who were all shouting, 'Hi, Bud!' or 'Hey, Jack!' and waving wads of money. Anne saw her young airman leaping into a taxi just ahead of her, but he avoided her eye, which served her right!

Poor, nice young man from Nebraska or Oklahoma, with a kind heart and the in-stincts of a gentleman, he would go through the rest of his life – if he survived the war –

thinking she was just another stuck-up Limey. He would never know that it was not pride but misery that made her disagreeable.

She did miss her train at Victoria, and when at last she was approaching Chichester, she had been traveling for more than nine hours – and she still had to face the final slow train. She remembered Mavis Bender saying, 'Why couldn't you get orff yer arse and meet me at Chichester?' and she began to smile, then found tears in her eyes. She was aware of the civil servant opposite who was eyeing her curiously over the pages of his evening paper, and she turned her face toward the window, seeing the pale shadow of her unhappiness reflected back.

If only they had never gone on that picnic, never had that awful quarrel! If only Tom could have been at the end of her journey – Tom, in any circumstance, on any terms! Anne felt such a surge of joy at the mere thought of it that the returning realization of the truth hit her heart like a stone. That week's leave, which had been intended to allow her to get her feelings under control, instead had only confirmed that she loved him, had sharpened the anguish of losing him, just as the pain of a violent injury is not

41

fully felt immediately but comes flooding in later as the soothing first aid pads are removed. Pride had come to help her at first, and shock had deadened the pain, but neither was of any use to her now. Worst of all was the knowledge that she would be seeing him almost every day, never talking or smiling, trying not to look for him, always aware of him coldly avoiding her.

The train drew in to Chichester, and the other people in the compartment got out. Anne stood up and busied herself with her case and her gas mask, afraid that someone might hold the door open for her or smile. Like someone who has suffered appalling burns, she felt that she could not bear to have any human being so much as lay a finger on her. When they had all gone, she turned toward the door and climbed down the high step. Her case was heavy – she had crammed in a couple of comforting Georgette Heyer novels at the last minute – and the strap of her gas mask holder cut into her shoulder. She had to walk the length of the platform in order to cross the line and catch the final slow train. Suddenly it seemed that this last part of that journey from nowhere to nothing was beyond human capacity – altogether beyond hers, at any rate. She took a deep breath and began to trudge toward the barrier. As she approached it, she saw an uniformed figure and knew that it was Tom. She put her case down and ran toward him. She was in his arms. Nobody else existed. Nothing else mattered.

'I had to come,' he said.

'Oh, Tom,' said Anne, 'I'm so glad!'

Four

'I wish,' said Anne.

'What?'

Tom had to lean his head toward her without seeming to, because the noise in the room had suddenly diminished. The landlord, Frank Baker, was telling one of his long and quite unintelligible stories, and the RAF lads gathered around the bar were gazing at him, baffled but benevolent. Only Jimmy Pratt, incurably optimistic, exclaimed, 'Oh, absolutely!' or 'Oh, wizard!' at intervals, in the hope that this might be the correct response.

'And the vicar, 'e says to me,' said Frank, '"you want to goo down Little Cobham," 'e says, "you won't find no vicar there," 'e says,

43

"'oo'll end 'is sermon to suit your opening time," 'e says!'

Frank roared with laughter, and his uninstructed audience laughed with him.

'I wish,' said Anne, 'that we'd gone to bed together.'

'Oh, darling!' said Tom. 'Thank you for saying that!'

Their hands clung together.

'Darling,' said Tom.

'Yes?'

'We could write, at least.'

'No,' said Anne, quickly and instinctively.

'Please,' said Tom. 'If we could write just one letter a year...'

'What good would that do?' demanded Anne, with a note of desperation.

'At least we'd be in touch!' replied Tom.

Anne could hear the suppressed violence in his voice. Her heart responded, but she fought back from the dangerous brink.

'That's just it,' she said. 'We'd be in touch. We'd be thinking about each other.'

'Don't you think we'll be doing that anyway?'

Again that surge of feeling, again that struggle to resist it.

'But we mustn't,' said Anne. 'Especially you. If you're thinking about me instead of Betty, you ... it wouldn't be fair to her.'

44

'I think,' said Tom, very coolly and precisely, 'I think that just once a year I might be allowed to think of you.'

Anne's other hand left her glass and came to clasp his between both of hers.

'I'd like that!' she said. 'Oh, I'd like that!'

She threw a quick glance at him.

'That's the trouble.'

Tom ignored her words and spoke quickly.

'That's settled then,' he said. 'One letter a year. Yes?'

'Oh, yes!' said Anne. She hesitated. 'How would we...?'

'Let's fix a time now,' said Tom. 'A date. How about today's date?'

Anne felt the weight on her heart lifting. Suddenly it was an adventure. Suddenly it was not all over.

'So every year,' she said, 'on July the twenty-fifth, we'd write to each other...'

'It would make more sense if we took it in turns to write a couple of days before,' said Tom. 'Then we could answer each other.'

'Oh no!' said Anne quickly. 'That wouldn't be right. We agreed... . That would mean that we weren't just thinking of each other. We'd be – we'd be communicating.'

'All right,' said Tom hastily. 'We'll both write once a year, on July the twenty-fifth.

45

We'll just – know we're thinking of each other.'

'Yes,' said Anne.

They were both silent for a moment, enjoying the thought of that foolish, romantic gesture that once a year would remind them of their love for each other.

'Won't Betty think it rather odd,' said Anne, 'this letter coming once a year from me?'

'She wouldn't have to know,' said Tom.

'But if the letter always came on the same day every year, and ... I mean she might get to know the handwriting and say, "That's funny. Here's that letter again," and you – what would you say?'

'I'd know when it was coming,' said Tom quickly. 'I'd get there first.'

'You mean, sneak down and...? That would be awful,' said Anne.

'Yes,' said Tom.

Anne took her other hand away.

'We can't do it,' she said.

'No,' said Tom, but he clung fast to her remaining hand.

The landlord came close to them, wiping tables and collecting glasses. The noisy chatter from the bar filled the silence between them.

'Can I get you anything while I'm 'ere?'

46

Frank Baker paused beside them, balancing a tray covered with beer mugs and dirty ashtrays.

'No thanks,' replied Tom. 'We're all right.' And as Frank moved away, he added, 'To coin a phrase.'

When they first agreed that they must part, the decision had seemed almost easy, not only because it was right, but because they were together. Somehow it had seemed as though making the decision together meant that they would not really be parted. And then, with the build-up to the invasion and the first of the flying bombs, it was a time of drama and excitement, and their own drama was part of it, illuminated by the romantic wartime glow of heroism and sacrifice. But now that the moment had arrived in all its bleak actuality...

'It is the same for you, isn't it?' said Tom.

'The same?'

'I mean, I wouldn't like to think that to you it was all just a romantic and charming episode...' He paused and added with unexpected fierceness, 'I want it to hurt you as much as it hurts me.'

Anne threw a startled glance at him and then turned her head away.

'Then you have your wish,' she said.

She felt his shoulder leaning against hers.

'I don't really,' he said.

'I know.'

'And yet I do.'

'I know,' said Anne. 'I feel the same. Isn't it odd? I was always brought up to think of love as something very sedate and respectable. You "fell in love" with someone frightfully suitable, and you walked in the garden together and gave each other bunches of flowers....'

'You never gave *me* a bunch of flowers,' said Tom, 'not even primroses...' and then, 'Oh, God!'

'Someone should have told me,' said Anne, 'that being in love was like this, that it wasn't something you felt gracefully and beautifully in your "heart."'

'You feel it in your guts,' said Tom.

'No, not exactly that, but ... yes, I suppose that's true.'

There was a heavy and slightly unfamiliar roar of a four-engine plane overhead, and they glanced up and then at each other.

'That damaged Lanc going home,' said Tom.

'Oh yes,' said Anne.

This time tomorrow, she thought, we shan't even share the war.

'Do you remember that airman,' she said, 'who fell out of a window onto the spiked

48

fence? They kept him alive for a week or two with sips of champagne, and then he died. Sitting here talking is the sips of champagne. And then you'll get up and go. And I'll die.'

'We'll both die,' said Tom.

Their hands clung painfully together. Tom's grip really hurt, but Anne was glad of it. Perhaps her fingers would be bruised, and she would feel them tomorrow and pretend that Tom was still holding her hand.

'You don't really think,' said Tom, 'that I can walk out of this pub and never see or hear of you again?'

'You must. We agreed.'

'Supposing Betty and I break up? We might, you know. People do.'

Anne freed her hand and spoke firmly.

'No,' she said. 'You won't. I don't want you to. And even if you did, it wouldn't make any difference.'

'You mean, even if I was free...'

'You wouldn't be,' said Anne. 'Not to me. I don't think you can turn marriage on and off like a light switch. I think once you take it on, it's like life: you're committed to it until you die. That's how it would've been for me, and I'm not going to make it less than that for Betty or for you.'

She lifted her glass to her lips and turned

49

to look at him.

'I love you too much for that.'

'You mean,' said Tom, 'if we'd loved each other less, there would've been more hope for us?'

'Oh, yes,' Anne answered readily. 'We could have written to each other, met again – perhaps even gone to bed together. It would have been – what did you say? – a romantic and charming episode, just another wartime romance. But as it is...'

She put her hand in his again, and felt gratefully the warmth of his clasp.

'We have to bury our love so deep,' she said, 'that we can never find it again, even if we want to.'

'I don't think I can,' said Tom.

'We must,' said Anne. 'Oh, darling, darling Tom, we must!'

Squadron Leader Bender turned away from the bar and headed for the door, giving them a friendly wave.

'Cheerio, Tom!' he called.

'Cheerio!' called Tom in reply.

The heavy oak door opened and swung shut.

'Cheerio,' said Tom. 'What a ridiculous expression!' He glanced at Anne.

'Do you want another drink?'

Anne shook her head.

'Frank has probably run out of gin by now anyway,' said Tom.

Bender's intervention had somehow lowered the emotional temperature.

'What do you think you'll do after the war?' asked Tom.

'I don't know,' answered Anne. It was hard to think of any kind of life after the war, and without Tom. 'I suppose I shall keep house for Daddy. He's had a rotten time since Mummy died, and he really – he really can't manage on his own.'

'You do realize,' said Tom, 'that I could come to Endersby and find you.'

'But you won't.'

'Damn it, there's a war on! The flying bombs are going to get worse, and you'll be in the thick of them – much more than I will. And it's quite likely Hitler'll try some desperation bombing of airfields. I must know you're still alive when the war's over!'

'Don't worry,' said Anne. 'I won't be.' She caught herself. 'Oh, I didn't mean to say that! I'll be alive and well, and you'll be alive and happy with Betty and the children, and we'll know that our love is there and we never spoiled it by using it to hurt other people. It'll be buried deep, and we'll never find it again, but we'll know it's there.'

'Oh, darling,' said Tom. 'Darling Anne, I

do love you so!'

They crouched a little and leaned toward each other, hand holding hand, shoulder touching shoulder. Jimmy Pratt and his fellow pilots were drifting toward the door, and Tom glanced at the clock over the bar.

'Oh, no!' cried Anne. 'It's not time yet! Oh, no!'

'Well...'

'Frank always keeps his clock fast – you know he does.'

'Yes,' said Tom. He looked toward the window and saw his car and driver waiting. 'And Jones drives like a maniac, but it's half an hour to the station, and...'

They stared at each other, suddenly aghast.

'It can't be – *time*!' said Anne. 'It can't be!'

'We must have been mad,' said Tom. 'Saying good-bye here – I can't even kiss you!'

Anne brought her other hand to join his and he clasped it so they clung together, invisibly, in a passionate embrace. Leaning toward him, Anne managed to put her cheek against his shoulder.

Tom stared straight ahead. 'Darling!' he said quietly. 'Oh, my darling!'

Anne sat up.

'You must go.'

'Yes.'

But as he began to draw his hands away, she held them tighter.

'I can't bear it!' she said. 'I can't bear it!'

They sat motionless. Cigarette smoke wreathed around Frank Baker's head as he washed glasses behind the bar. An aircraft droned overhead.

'It's all right,' said Anne desperately. 'I know you must go.'

'I'll take the next train,' said Tom.

'No,' said Anne. 'It's never going to get any better.'

'Darling,' said Tom. 'It's all I can say, somehow, darling.'

'Yes.'

They were incredulous again. Tom drew his hands away and stood up.

'I suppose...' he said absurdly.

'Yes,' said Anne.

He hesitated, went toward the door, and turned. They stared at each other, and then he opened the door and was gone. Anne half rose, turning toward the window to catch a final glimpse, but he had walked the other way. She sank back in her seat and raised her glass, pretending to drink the dregs of her gin and lime, hoping to conceal the tears running down her cheeks. He was gone. She would never see him again, never as long as she lived.

Five

'Betty!' called Tom.

He slammed the door behind him and put his umbrella in the stand and his bowler hat on its peg. From upstairs he heard children's voices and the splashing of water. His wife came out on the landing, her dark curly hair untidy and her cheeks flushed. She wore a big apron over her dress, and Lucy ran out after her in her blue flannel dressing gown and bare feet.

'Daddy! Daddy!'

She started down the stairs, and Tom went up to meet her, catching her in his arms. She smelled of Johnson's baby powder, and the hair on the back of her neck was wet. She gave him a big hug, and he was surprised, as he always was, by the strength of feeling she put into it. She was such a funny little girl, with her silky fair hair and wiry body and that way she had of keeping her feelings close inside her and then, very occasionally, exploding into wild screaming

54

fits that left them alarmed and her exhausted. And those explosions were always over some trivial matter, as though it was a token of deeper emotions that she did not let them see, just as now she hugged him in silence. Colin, on the other hand, round-faced and tubby, expressed his feelings with the greatest alacrity at all times.

'How did it go?' asked Betty, but half her mind was on a shrill screech and splash from the bathroom.

Tom looked up at her over Lucy's head.

'Not too bad,' he answered. 'It was a bit like a briefing really. I'm not sure I've taken it all in.'

'I'll make you a pot of tea,' said Betty. 'You can finish putting them to bed.'

'Oh – right,' said Tom.

He would have preferred it the other way around. He was never quite sure how the children felt about him, especially Colin, who was born in 1943, after a rather splendid leave in Dorset, when he and Betty recaptured the mysterious honeymoon sensation that transforms the matrimonial bed into a romantic adventure. Lucy, at least, was old enough to understand that he had to be away from them because of the war (whatever she understood the war to be), but when he corrected Colin for some disobedience or impudence, he sometimes surprised a look in his eye that was dismaying in so young a child and that clearly said, 'Who is this interloper?' On the other hand, Tom found that four years in the Royal Air Force had left him singularly unfit for domestic duties. Meals had been put in front of him, cups of tea summoned at a word. It was easier to put the children to bed than to make himself a pot of tea.

Tom went into the bathroom and saw Colin sitting in the bath looking disconcertingly like a naked miniature of himself.

'Right, old chap,' he said with false jollity, 'out you come!'

Colin instantly raised a rabbit-shaped sponge and squeezed a stream of water over Tom's suit.

With Lucy's help, Tom got Colin out of the bath and more or less dry and into his pyjamas, though the bathroom looked like the deck of the *Titanic* just before it finally went down.

'Come on,' he said hopefully. 'Into bed, and Mummy will come up and read you a story.'

He headed for the small bedroom but was stopped in his tracks by an agonized roar from behind him.

'What happened?' Horrified, he turned

56

back, knelt down, and took hold of the little boy who stood on the landing, howling. 'Did you hurt yourself?'

He searched for blood, for a bruise.

'Peter!' screamed Colin through his tears. 'I want Peter!'

'Who's Peter?'

'It's his blanket,' explained Lucy solemnly.

'I thought that was George.'

'It was George *yesterday*,' said Lucy reproachfully.

'Oh, for God's sake!' said Tom, standing up, and met Betty's reproving eye as she came up the stairs and bent over Colin.

'Here you are, darling,' she said. 'I had to wash Peter, he was so dirty.'

'He doesn't *like* being washed!' bellowed Colin, but he clutched the ragged object to his small bosom and stumped off, sucking one corner of it, his tears miraculously vanished.

'It's really like a dummy,' said Tom. 'Except that he keeps calling it by different names. Isn't he getting a bit old for that sort of thing?'

He got another reproving look, and caught a slightly wounded reflection of it in Lucy's face.

'Your tea's in the sitting room,' said Betty.

Tom sank down in the armchair, feeling

57

the knees of his trousers clammy with bath-water. He hated that suit. He knew that his dislike had its origins in snobbery and that made him dislike it still more. The material was shoddy, and it creased easily, but even more he missed the kudos that he had derived from his well-cut officer's uniform – the same natural, if absurd, benefit that one would derive from being a lord.

'Yes, sir. Certainly, sir,' everyone had said, just as they said, 'Yes, m'lord.'

But there was one vital difference: his officer's status had been strictly temporary, whereas even a down-and-out aristocrat preserved a certain *cachet*. What was worse, he found, back in Civvy Street, his wartime experience was of no real benefit to him. He had not even been a fighting man. Everyone insisted that the 'glamour boys' had a hard time finding work. They should have tried *not* being glamour boys, thought Tom bitterly, remembering the number of times he had heard the jovial words: 'RAF, eh? What did you fly? Spitfires? Lancasters?'

'Er – no. My eyesight wasn't good enough. I was a controller.'

'Ah.' And then, 'Right. We'll let you know.'

Mr Osmund, after many disappointments, had proved to be the exception.

'Have to keep your wits about you for that,

58

I shouldn't wonder,' he said.

Mr Osmund had been in the army, and had used his gratuity to set himself up in a small firm selling office equipment. (Lucky devil! thought Tom. He himself had had to spend his gratuity in buying a house.) Mr Osmund had a notion that, now the war was over, Britain was bound to get back into business, especially when it got rid of Attlee and 'them bloody Socialists.' Mr Osmund was born in the East End of London and therefore was determinedly Conservative in his politics – or, at least, he was strongly in favour of private enterprise.

'Stands to reason,' he said, 'people set up in business, they want office furniture. And, the war being over, bound to be some army surplus. What we have to do is to put the two together.'

Tom had more than half a notion that Mr Osmund himself might have been in the quartermaster's department and had useful access to this very 'army surplus,' but he really felt that was none of his business. What mattered was that Mr Osmund was prepared to offer him a job as a salesman at a salary which would enable him to pay the mortgage on the house, with enough left over to live on. How ironic, he thought, pouring the tea from the small brown teapot, that one should give four years of one's life to fighting the appalling evil of Nazism and end up doing a job for which one was not in the least suited but which would at least pay the mortgage!

'Their shoulders held the skies suspended.
They stood and earth's foundations stay.
What God abandoned, these defended—
And now the bloody mortgage pay!'

Tom leaned back in his chair, holding the cup as if it were a tin mug and sipping the welcome hot tea. He thought of Betty's reproving look when he said, 'Oh, for God's sake!' and remembered Anne saying, 'Please don't swear,' and his heart gave that all-too-familiar lurch in his chest.

He was like a man in an H. G. Wells novel who had been swept away from his ordinary life and suddenly plonked down on a strange planet and who couldn't get back to his real life again. Only his real life was the war and that well-fitting uniform and the job in the control room, which he had so completely mastered – and Anne.

'You really do love me, don't you?' Betty had said to him once not long before the war. 'It wasn't just that you wanted to get married, and I happened to come along?'

60

'Of course not,' said Tom irritably, but he was lying.

He *had* wanted to get married. He was tired of living in his parents' house in Streatham. He wanted a wife of his own to go to bed with and a home of his own and children. Betty was there, and they danced well together, and when he kissed her, she kissed him back and was warm and affectionate and – most dangerous aphrodisiac of all – she made it clear that she loved him.

So there he was, tied by the toe in a flat in Clapham, with a pretty girl he liked but who got on his nerves sometimes, with a draughtsman's job that didn't really suit him, and he felt that there must be something more in life, but he couldn't think what it could be – that is, until the war came, and Anne. And now he was back again, tied by the toe once more, only this time he was in a shabby suit in a bomb-damaged house in Balham, and this time he had two children he hardly knew, and this time it was worse, much worse, because he had known what it was to be free, and because he had met the one girl in the whole world whom he could love with all his heart, and he could never have her. She was removed from him as completely as if she lived in another time or on another planet,

61

and he would never see her again as long as he lived.

Tom put his cup down and sat forward, clasping his arms across his stomach and shivering a little, as a man might when left alone in a prison cell. Then he became aware that he was no longer alone. Betty had come silently down the carpeted stairs (utility carpet, of course!) and into the room, and he caught a look of puzzlement in her dark eyes. He sat back in the chair.

'It's bloody cold in here,' he said.

'I wish you wouldn't swear,' said Betty, 'especially in front of the children.'

Six

'Look at those chilblains,' said Jean, holding her hands out over the tiny grate and the dim blue flame. 'It's disgusting. I haven't had chilblains since I was nine – and it was disgusting then.'

'This will go down in history,' said Anne, 'as the year when Eskimos and polar bears roamed the streets of Cambridge, and the Eskimos' noses froze and fell off...'

'And the polar bears ate them,' completed Sarah.

'Never mind the polar bears, *I'd* eat them!' said Freda. 'I'm starving!'

They all laughed. The four girls were drinking cocoa, huddled over the remains of the fire in Freda's room above the archway. They had pooled their one scuttle of coal per day, and even that was nearly gone.

'The first thing I'm going to do when I get home,' said Anne, 'is to go wooding.'

'Bring some back with you,' urged Jean. 'Leave the Chaucer behind. Next term might be even colder.'

They all groaned.

'It can't be,' said Anne. 'Anyway, I shall probably need it in Norfolk. My father said he went into the church last week and the font was frozen.'

'What did he break the ice with? The baby's head?'

They all laughed again, and Anne laughed, disgracefully, with them. It was like being back at school, she thought. Or rather, since she had never enjoyed school much, it was like having a family, with all the family jokes and family loyalties. She looked around at her friends. Freda was tall, with regular features, her dark hair drawn back in a bun. She was majoring in science, and they knew

63

that she was by far the most brilliant of them all, though she never seemed to work. She had an unholy passion for children's books because her father was a physicist and her mother a chemist, and they never had a book in the house that was not solidly based on fact. 'Imagination' to them simply meant 'not proven' or 'not true.' Freda, coming upon *The Wind in the Willows* and *Curly and the Goblins* in her twenties, was enraptured by them far more than any child, while the final chapters of *Little Lord Fauntleroy* had her sobbing her heart out.

The bitter wind from the fens howled through the small, ill-fitting window, and Jean groaned again.

'Ugh! Just think – this time tomorrow, I'll be in Durham. Why should I go to Durham? Who lives in Durham?'

'Your parents.'

'But *why*?'

'Because they were born there.'

'Why didn't they move?'

'Perhaps they like it there.'

'They do!' moaned Jean. 'That's the worst of it. They'll have all the family round to admire the first of the Armstrongs who ever went to university, and they'll all say, "Haway, Hinney!" and ask me if I read a lot of books.'

'Don't they know you're studying mathematics?' inquired Sarah solicitously.

'And that mathematicians can't read,' finished Anne.

'That's enough from you, Hawthorne!' said Jean in the tones of the WREN officer that she had once been. Thin and wiry, with an olive complexion, she had a hint of the north country in her vowels and the way she rolled her Rs. 'Just think of that journey tomorrow,' she said. 'Nine hours in an unheated train, with nothing to eat. Ugh! The font may be frozen, but at least you've got quite a short journey.'

'Yes,' said Anne.

'A short journey,' she thought, 'but no Tom at the end of it.'

Her face fell into misery.

'Now then, Anne,' said Freda. 'You're thinking about the man that got away.'

They all laughed, and Anne was glad to laugh with them. Freda had invented the joke. They were all at Newnham on their ex-service grants and had somehow gravitated together. It was Freda who identified the fact that they were all quite attractive but not married because the man they could have loved was killed or crippled or went abroad at the wrong time or was married. She herself had been an ATS officer in a

65

small unit that the others suspected to have been a highly secret intelligence unit, and she had fallen in love with her CO. He was dark and handsome, with charming manners, and despite the fact that he and Freda worked so closely together, he seemed to have no idea that she was falling in love with him. On D-Day he flew into France, and his glider crashed and broke both his legs and his back. He went home to his wife, and Freda never saw him again. In a curious way, it made it worse that he was crippled because she loved him so much that it would have given her pure joy just to be with him, whereas she suspected that his elegant, aristocratic wife would be exasperated and impatient. Sarah, small, blonde, and pretty, a year or two younger than the rest of them, lost her childhood sweetheart at Arnhem, and Jean's fiancé had been lost at sea. Anne, the memory of her destructive love affair still vivid, was glad to know that, however tragic a love affair might be, one could still laugh at it in the right company.

Anne loved Cambridge. It was easy to love it in the spring, with daffodils growing all along the Backs, and easier still in the early summer. She and Jean had spent magic afternoons, reclining in a punt while one shirt-sleeved undergraduate punted them up the Cam and another read aloud from the *Book of Comic Verse* to lazy but convulsive giggles. Some eager young girls, straight from school, punted themselves energetically about, presumably with the hope of catching the men's admiring attention.

'Very jolly hockeysticks!' said Peter Piddock scathingly and then, running along the punt, trailing the pole, ran right off the end of it into the river.

There were a lot of good-natured fellows like Peter, whom one or other of the 'Family' had picked up at a lecture or already knew from home, and they shared them like headscarves or lecture notes. They all used to gather in the Copper Kettle, amid a swirl of shabby black gowns, yelling greetings across the room and making up little parties to go to the Arts Theatre or the movies, having dinner first at the K. P. Restaurant. Anne saw *Les Enfants du Paradis* five times, until she knew the dialogue by heart, but she only went to *Hamlet* once, since, when the unfortunate actor uttered the immortal words, 'To sleep, perchance to dream!' Freda remarked, *sotto voce*, 'Just like Ivor Novello!' and they all got such frightful giggles that they had to go out.

But if Cambridge was at its best in the summer, Anne found that she loved it

67

almost as much in the winter, despite the perishing cold and the one scuttle of coal per day and the continuing food rationing. She enjoyed bicycling down Sidgewick Avenue to the flock of bicycles and torn gowns outside the lecture rooms in Mill Lane. She even enjoyed the lectures, though they weren't very good, except for Rylands and Professor Sykes, who was really a professor of divinity, but who used splendidly illuminating cricketing metaphors about Cranmer keeping a straight bat and Queen Elizabeth bowling googlies. The worst lecturer by far was unfortunately Anne's Newnham tutor, an anxious and introverted girl of about her own age, who had gone straight from school to university, stayed on doing post-graduate research, and now, having missed all the experiences of her contemporaries in the wide, wartime world, was a calamitously dull don and a learned and deadly boring lecturer, with a rapidly diminishing audience.

'Come along,' Anne would say, 'who's going to poor Dr Parsons's lecture today? Spenser's *Faerie Queen*. It'll be *awful*. We must get a quorum. Sarah?'

'I went last week. Come on, Freda, it's your turn.'

'I'm not even studying English!'

68

'Never mind, take *Little Lord Fauntleroy* with you, and look up every so often and laugh at her jokes.'

'She doesn't make jokes.'

'Yes, she does,' said Jean, 'but nobody notices them. Just laugh, and she'll think she's said something witty. It'll encourage her no end.'

Going to Cambridge had almost been an accident for Anne. She had been advised that an ex-service grant would pay for her further education and, struggling against the certainty that her life was over, applied for one, much as a man lost in a dark wood will take any path that offers the hope that it will lead him out of it. Now that she was there, it seemed that getting an honors degree in English was something that, for the first time in her life, she was doing because *she* wanted to do it and not just because it was expected of her. Fortunately, though, her father had gone to Jesus College, Cambridge, and therefore felt very much at ease with the notion of a daughter who was, however belatedly, an undergraduate.

'Do you know what you want to do, my dear,' her father asked mildly, 'after you leave Cambridge?'

'No, not really,' Anne replied.

They were eating their celebratory first-night meal of bacon and a real egg.

'It's just nice to think of having a degree – being qualified for something, even if I never use it.'

She saw the troubled look on her father's face and added hastily, 'And Professor Sykes suggested that I might write a thesis on Bunyan. You've got a marvelous Bunyan library. I could write it here.'

She saw her father's look of relief and pleasure and was well rewarded.

'Yes,' he said. 'Yes, I suppose you could.'

It was good, after all, to be sleeping again in her bare, cold bedroom in the eighteenth-century rectory, full of echoes of Nelson and Jane Austen, even though it was so cold that the hot water bottle that she hugged when she went to bed gurgled chillily against her when she woke up – and she woke early because she was stiff with the cold. She went downstairs and raked out the wood-burning stove in the kitchen. They used to have a huge iron coal stove, with a large iron kettle continually simmering on it, but she had persuaded her father to invest in the wood stove after Gladys left. It was cheaper than the coal stove but still caused him some conscience searching, because he

70

thought he ought to spend the money on the damp in the north transept of the church instead. It was probably the first time that Anne had stood firm against her father. What a victory, she thought, to have won a wood stove and fuel that did not take a laborer's strength to carry in from the coalshed outside the back door! Still, they had constant hot water now and, as long as you remembered to open up the stove half an hour before you wanted it and were prepared to juggle saucepans from the hot to the cool areas, quite good cooking possibilities. Anne remembered with a hungry sigh the steak and kidney puddings that Mrs Barber used to make before the war, and moved the kettle on to the hot ring and settled down to the kitchen table to work.

She was glad that she was studying *Piers Plowman* and not Chaucer. She had never liked Chaucer much. All those dirty stories – ugh! – interspersed with romantic poetry that was rather finicky. Chaucer was a townee and a courtier, and she much preferred Langland, with his mixture of hardworking country life and the Christian allegory. Professor Sykes had laughed when she told him this.

'You're a puritan, Miss Hawthorne,' he said, his eyes twinkling beneath his bushy

71

dark eyebrows.

'Yes,' answered Anne, amused. 'If that means believing in the truth, the whole truth, and nothing but the truth, I think I am.'

'Ah,' he replied, 'pride, Miss Hawthorne, pride is the besetting sin of all puritans.'

They laughed at each other, and Anne smiled at the thought of it now, as she set to work in the warm kitchen. A robin sang outside the window in the winter jasmine, and Anne felt an unexpected surge of pleasure, such as she had never thought to feel again. She loved her friends at Newnham, loved them like sisters – and they were like the family she had never had, sharing experiences with a candor that was new to her and probably to them. It had been a joy, too, to discover that she had a good academic brain, and that she took pleasure in using it. That gave her an independence she had never thought to possess. She could earn her own living, and enjoy doing so, without feeling the need for love or marriage. She listened to the robin's song in the chill dawn and felt a tiny warm glow of life within her, like the minute green shoot of life that struggles out through the dead wood of winter. She was so grateful to be aware of that spirit of hope that she had never expected to feel again that she resolved to go to church that morning, partly to say thank you and partly to mark the beginning of a new life, a life without Tom.

The rector said Matins in the church every morning at ten o'clock, winter and summer, Monday to Saturday. He had done so ever since he was ordained, and no doubt he would continue to do so until he died. Usually there was no one else there except for the occasional devoted spinster or a visitor who had come to view the architecture and gotten trapped into being the sole member of the congregation in an all-too-unexpected service, with the rector courteously but disconcertingly waiting for mumbled and belated responses. This morning he and Anne were alone, and she found the calm and splendid words of the *Book of Common Prayer* wonderfully uplifting. While her father prayed silently at the altar, she glanced ahead through the collects and found one that, as usual, was perfectly appropriate.

'O Almighty God, who alone canst order the unruly wills and affections of sinful men, grant unto thy people that they may love the thing which thou commandest, and desire that which thou dost promise, that so among the sundry and manifold changes of

73

the world, our hearts may surely there be fixed where true joys are to be found.'

No more unruly wills and affections, thought Anne, and drew a deep breath, as though she had laid down a burden that was too heavy for her to carry.

When the service was over, Anne sat still for a moment in the comfortably familiar rectory pew. Her father returned from the vestry.

'I must go and see Mrs Beecham this morning,' he said. 'She was very poorly last week. I'd better go straight along now. The doctor was coming today, and she might have to go into hospital.'

'All right, Daddy,' called Anne. 'I'll just fill the flowers up.'

She always enjoyed the small domestic chores in the church, and this morning she enjoyed it more than ever, feeling that it was an offering of thanks for her newfound freedom. A bunch of frozen daffodil buds had died prematurely in their vase on the pulpit, and Anne unhooked the green metal flower holder and took it out through the vestry to replace them. She threw the dead flowers on the usual rather disreputable little rubbish dump behind the church and turned toward the water tank. It would probably be frozen hard, but if so, she could

74

find a stone and break the ice. Her mind entirely upon that absurd little problem, she turned the corner and saw Tom. He was standing with his back to her, looking up at the church tower, a stocky figure in civilian clothes, hatless, with light brown hair. Anne couldn't move. She could hardly breathe. This was how people died of joy. He had come. Tom had come, and nothing else mattered.

The rapture lasted only a second. He turned and saw her and came toward her. It wasn't Tom. It was a stranger. He was Tom's build, his hair was the same color, but he was younger, and his eyes were blue.

'Excuse me,' he said. 'Is the church open?'

'Oh – yes,' said Anne. 'We never lock it in the daytime.'

'Splendid!' he said, glancing at the guide-book in his hand. 'Thanks awfully!'

He hastened toward the porch. Anne stood motionless, holding the ridiculous green metal flower holder, its rusty leaks inadequately soldered. It had all been a delusion. She loved Tom. She loved him still. She would love him until she died.

Seven

'Come on, everyone,' said Jean, sitting down at the long table, 'who's going to a May Ball? Someone must, for the honor of the Family.'

It had become their custom to hold their Family conferences over breakfast, always sitting in the same seats, as if in some imaginary women officers' mess.

'Sarah's going to the Boat Race Ball,' Anne protested.

'That doesn't count,' said Freda. 'It's much too eccentric.'

Sarah had spent her three years at Cambridge going out with a member of the Cambridge boat crew – or rather, since he was in training, *not* going out with him. Going out with Derek consisted of standing for hours by the Cam until at last he appeared, puce in the face, wearing a vest gray with sweat and river water and rowing in the wrong direction while a dwarf in the front of the boat yelled at him, and a giant who rode on a bicycle along a towpath roared through a megaphone, scattering all bystanders including Sarah and those loyal members of the Family who had toiled along in her support. They did not include Freda, who thought the whole thing was a ghastly mistake.

'So,' said Jean, 'apart from Sarah...?'

'Charles Prendergast asked me to go to the Trinity Ball,' said Anne.

They all looked at her.

'Only yesterday,' she added apologetically.

She had met Charles at a tea party in Peter Piddock's rooms in Pembroke and liked him on sight. He was a tall ex-Guards Officer, limping slightly from having ridden his motorbike incautiously over a land mine in the desert. He had blue eyes and slightly tousled fair hair, and because she found him so attractive, Anne instinctively drew back. She was surprised when he asked her to go on the river with him the next day, but she accepted and found his company very restful. He punted her up to Grantchester for tea and then back again, and they talked very little. Anne thought that perhaps it was because he was so handsome and because so many girls made a play for him that he was glad to be in the company of a girl who was content to allow him to make the

77

moves, and who didn't care too much whether he did or didn't. He took her to the movies, and afterward to a small Greek restaurant, where, he told her, he had heard that they served excellent steaks. He was absolutely right, but one bite of the unusually sweet and tender meat was enough to convince Anne that it was horse. She looked at Charles's happily triumphant face and remembered Tom saying, 'I love an innocent and trusting nature,' and her heart turned over. Perhaps that was why, when Charles asked her to go with him to the Trinity Ball, she accepted.

'Charles Prendergast,' said Jean thoughtfully. 'Sounds a bit too good to be true. Do you think he's a con man?'

'Very likely,' answered Anne.

'No, he isn't,' said Sarah. 'Derek knows him. His father's a bishop, and his uncle's a duke.'

'A touch above our style,' said Jean.

'That's all right,' said Anne. 'I don't really want to go anyway.'

They eyed her severely.

'Of course you must go,' said Jean, 'for the honor of the Family.'

They all helped her to dress, with Sarah's stole and fan and Jean's evening bag and Freda's string of pearls. Anne, looking at

78

herself in the narrow mirror, couldn't help knowing that she looked rather nice.

'I feel like an idiot,' she said. 'May Balls are for debs.'

'Never mind,' said Jean. 'It's bound to be better than mine.'

Jean had accepted a last-minute invitation from a scientist called Dougal to go to a May Ball the night before.

'It was unbelievable!' she reported on her return. 'There he was, a Scotsman, and he was cheap – such a cliché!'

'Perhaps he is hard up,' said Sarah.

'In that case,' replied Jean, 'he should have brought sandwiches, and we could have had a picnic, but to take me out to dinner at the University Arms and leave a sixpenny tip...! I didn't know whether to nip back and put down an extra ten bob or to sweep out and pretend I hadn't noticed.'

'Sweep out,' said Anne. 'You'll never dare go back anyway. Might as well save the ten bob.'

They all giggled like schoolgirls.

'Taxi's here,' said Freda, peering out the window. 'And your very elegant-looking gent, all white tie and tails.'

'Oh, no!' Anne groaned.

In spite of the jokes, Anne really did feel uneasy. It was a general, if unspoken,

79

assumption that accepting an invitation to a May Ball denoted a promise. Quite how much was promised was never altogether certain, but a promise of some kind was definitely implied. Of course, if the man was an idiot or a creep who would be lucky to get a partner at all, one needn't feel too badly if one just made use of him, but she really liked Charles, and he had made it very clear that he liked her. But, after all, she thought as she emerged from beneath the arch and saw him smiling at her, he was old enough to look after himself – and she would have hated to leave Cambridge without having been to a May Ball.

It was, in fact, a delightful evening. The other couples in the party were all cheerful and agreeable, with only one rather debby girl from London, who remarked in the ladies' room, 'I say, you're one of those blue-stockings, aren't you?'

The marquee, the champagne, and the salmon all made Anne feel that the war was over at last and that it was allowable to be frivolous and lighthearted – even, perhaps, irresponsible. At first they all danced and talked and laughed interchangeably, but after supper, as the music became more romantic, Anne danced only with Charles and found him a charming and amusing

80

companion. That is, until about three in the morning, when she suddenly said, 'Oh, how awful!'

He looked at her inquiringly.

'I'm enjoying myself so much,' she said, 'but...'

'But?'

She felt the familiar ache behind her eyes and the stone-heavy indigestion of fatigue.

'I'm exhausted. It suddenly feels like night duty!'

He began to laugh, too, and put his arm around her waist.

'Would you like to come and lie down on my bed and have a nap?'

'Oh, that would be marvelous!'

'Then we'll punt up the river to Grantchester and see the sun rise and have breakfast.'

They went together up the stone spiral staircase. All around them in that sternly masculine building were the sounds of women's voices and giggles, and the odd petal from a wilting corsage lay on the stairs. Charles opened the door to his room with a certain pride. Clearly, he had been at some pains to tidy it up, and there was even a bunch of roses stuck bolt upright in an exceedingly ugly vase that Anne suspected had been bought for the occasion. But there was something touching in the fact that a solitary man's room, however heroically tidied and especially if the man had been in the army like Charles, always had the air of a slightly sordid barracks.

'Mm,' said Anne, looking around, 'very nice.'

Charles beamed, and with the same naive and earnest domesticity, he concentrated on turning the bedcovers back. Anne lay down on the bed. She could not pretend to feel astonished when he knelt down beside her and took her in his arms.

'Anne, darling Anne!' he said, and kissed her.

'Oh well, here goes!' thought Anne, and put her arms around him and kissed him back.

It was easy at first to respond. She liked him so much, and she wanted so much to be loved. And then, as his passion increased, it was as though her mind acquiesced but it was her body which refused to yield. She struggled against him, and at once he freed her.

'No!' she said.

She saw the shocked look in his eyes and put her head against his shoulder.

'Oh, Charles, I can't! I thought I could but I can't! I'm so sorry. There's someone I love.

Someone I met in the war. I'm so sorry.'

She raised her head and saw his rueful smile.

'It's all right,' he said. 'Bless you for being so honest.'

He kissed her very gently on the cheek and stood up.

'Go to sleep.'

'He was a perfect gent,' said Anne, telling a slightly edited version of the story to the Family next day.

'You mean,' said Jean, 'that he didn't say, "I've wasted a lot of money on you!" Dougal did.'

'Nothing like it,' replied Anne. 'He came back and woke me up at five o'clock, and we punted up to Grantchester and met the others for breakfast. I don't know what *they* thought.'

'The worst!' said the Family, with one voice.

'That deb,' remarked Freda thoughtfully, 'did you say her name was Annabel? She's quite well known among the chaps. They call her Colman.'

'Colman?'

'Because she's as sharp as mustard.'

They all collapsed into laughter, and Anne was glad to laugh, too. It was only to Jean she confided that when Charles brought her back to Newnham, he kissed her, very gently, on the lips, and said, 'Good-bye, my dear.'

'It was because of the man that got away, wasn't it?' said Jean accusingly.

'Look who's talking!' said Anne.

She remembered Jean's young man from Gateshead who joined the RNVR and went down on convoy duty in the Atlantic. But at least Jean had gone to bed with Graham on the night before he sailed. All her anti-Durham jokes were to cover the bitter disappointment she felt at not having his baby, however horrified her family might have been. Anne knew how she felt. If only she could have had Tom's child! But then she thought what an appalling effect that would have had on her father, what anguish it would have caused him and, even if they could have ignored the local gossip, how difficult it would have been to bring up an illegitimate child in the small Norfolk village on an aging rector's salary. So perhaps it was all for the best, thought Anne, if only she could forget Tom. If only she could stop loving him.

Eight

Those first months at Osmund's were the worst of Tom's life. They were worse than the first days after his call-up, when he realized that neither being the only son of fond parents with one affectionate sister, nor his brief married life with a loving and houseproud wife, had prepared him for communal life with fellow airmen whose personal habits seemed to have been learned in the assorted slum areas of the British Isles. But at least he knew that would not last for more than a few weeks. Osmund's was even worse than the time he spent after leaving school, when he worked as a draughtsman, knowing it was the wrong career, because then he had some hope of escaping into something better. Now there was no escape. He needed the salary and desperately needed the commissions. There was a mortgage to pay and a family to support.

His early suspicion that he was not cut out

85

to be a salesman had been painfully re-inforced with every day that passed. He was acutely embarrassed because Mr Osmund had insisted that he should have cards printed with his name and RAF rank. (He had to pay for them himself, too.) Heaven only knew what the businessmen he visited expected when they read 'Flight Lieutenant Thomas Percival Sanders. Sales Executive, Osmund Office Equipment.' It certainly cannot have been a rather ordinary-looking man in a crumpled suit trying to hawk cheap army surplus. The worst of it was that the men who greeted him – no, they didn't greet him – they looked up at him with fishy eyes, holding his card between finger and thumb, and they were sitting at desks. If a man was in business, he had to have a desk. That was the first thing he bought. Tom wasn't only trying to sell refrigerators to Eskimos. He was trying to sell refrigerators to Eskimos who already *had* refrigerators.

He found that his best hope was to sit on the edge of the secretary's desk (yes, the secretaries had desks, too!) and try to per-suade her that her working life would be made easier if she had some additional office furniture. The knowledge that if he succeeded, the table, chair or filing cabinet that was delivered would be cheap and nasty and instantly recognized as such by her employer who would have to pay for it, did not give him much pleasure in the few sales that he did manage to achieve.

Then, after that wearying and humiliating round, home he would go in the crowded train to the horrid little house, where Betty was irritable and Colin was noisy and Lucy was quiet, and where, sitting over the small brown teapot, he had time to feel ashamed of wishing that the war was still on and that he was among friends, doing the work he knew and did well, for the sake of something he believed in.

'Tom, you look awful,' said his sister Pauli when they were having lunch together in a milk bar near the office, because he was paying and couldn't afford anything else. 'You and Betty ought to take a holiday.'

'I'm not due a holiday yet.'

'I don't care – you ought to pack the children off to Mum and Dad and get away together, just the two of you.'

'It wouldn't be much good,' Tom answered. 'We haven't anything to say to each other.'

'All the more reason,' said Pauli. 'When David came back from the desert, I couldn't even remember the color of his eyes. He insisted on going off to Scotland because he

87

said he wanted a bit of peace and quiet. I don't think we uttered anything for the first week, and then it got so boring, we had to start talking to each other because there was no one else to talk to except the fish – and he wasn't having much luck with *them*!' Her voice softened. 'He told me all about Tobruk and how frightened he'd been. One night he talked until five in the morning, and I didn't say a word, just listened. That's what you and Betty ought to do.'

She looked at Tom. He was staring at the coffee-stained table, remembering how he had sat quite still in the car holding Anne in his arms, the night they decided that they must part. Driving back from the movies, he had stopped the car in a country lane, and they kissed. They very nearly consummated their love, there in the car, but struggled back from the brink of uncontrollable passion, and Anne clung to him and cried. Tom was flooded with that protective tenderness that alone is stronger than passion and that perhaps, in the end, distinguishes men from animals.

'Don't cry. Darling, please don't cry.'

'It's wrong,' Anne sobbed. 'I want it so much, but I know it's wrong!'

He wiped her eyes and smoothed her hair, and they sat and talked. They talked until they reached the irrefutable conclusion that they could not build their happiness on other people's misery, and that they loved each other so much that if they stayed close together, they must take the last step where love found its physical fulfillment. They decided that one of them must ask for a transfer. Then, talked out, they sat motionless in each other's arms, knowing that their minds were one mind, their hearts one heart, their bodies essentially one body, until dawn came and the first bird twittered and they stirred and looked at each other, pale as ghosts, and knew they must go back on duty and that their parting had begun.

'Tom?' said Pauli.

He looked up at her.

'It's not the same,' he said.

He saw Pauli hesitate, half inclined to ask more, and was relieved when she didn't.

'Now, come along, Tom,' she said, with that firm conviction of right that an elder sister never quite loses. 'David's got some leave in a couple of months, and we're going to rent a cottage in Dorset. It's by the sea, quite near Weymouth, so Mum and Dad can take all the children off our hands now and then, but the important thing is we'll all be together, and you'll get used to being in the family again. David says that's the hardest part.'

Tom wondered if his brother-in-law had met any one special girl during his four years' absence in North Africa, Italy, and Normandy, and decided he'd better not go into that.

Pauli picked up her gloves and handbag. She had always been a handsome girl, but since she married David, she had acquired that indefinable air of country elegance that comes from buying very few clothes but always of the finest quality. Her hair, no longer a rashly dyed auburn, was now her own sedate brown, and only the lively hazel eyes betrayed the unregenerate Pauli behind the proper regular army wife.

'I must catch my train,' she said. 'Now, come on, Tom. Betty needs a holiday, too, you know.'

'Yes, I know,' answered Tom wearily. It was easier to agree than to argue anymore. 'Osmund hasn't even mentioned holidays yet. I'll ask him this afternoon.'

In any event, Tom didn't get around to mentioning holidays that afternoon. Sitting at his (army surplus) desk, Mr Osmund studied Tom's weekly report and then looked up at him.

'If things go on at this rate,' he said, 'we're going to have to cut our sales force.'

'Our sales force only consists of Harry Bridges and me,' said Tom.

Mr Osmund eyed him thoughtfully.

'That's right,' he said ominously.

Tom, traveling in the crowded train, with an elbow in his ribs and an attaché case jammed into his calf, could only be thankful that it was the weekend and he wouldn't have to set out again the next morning trying to sell the unsalable, knowing with a new and painful urgency that his job depended on it.

It had become the habit when he got home for Lucy to be there to greet him, running out of the bathroom or her bedroom or the sitting room, according to the time. This evening he was a little earlier than usual, and there was no sign of her. He was glancing around with a surprisingly keen sense of disappointment, when she jumped out at him.

'I say!' he exclaimed. 'That nearly made me jump out of my skin. It must be Tigger.'

'Yes!' she replied, delighted. 'It is. It's Tigger!'

They were reading *The House at Pooh Corner*, which Tom had never read in his childhood, but in which he now took an illicit pleasure because Anne had said it was one of her favourites.

'Did you have a good day, Daddy?' inquired Lucy.

She was echoing the words she had heard her mother use; with Betty it was slightly perfunctory, whereas Lucy asked the question with a solemn earnestness that demanded a serious reply.

'Not very good,' said Tom. 'Nobody thought I was very clever today, not even your Aunt Pauli.'

'Tiggers don't care,' said Lucy. 'Tiggers love you anyway.'

'So they do,' said Tom and, stooping down, put his arms around her and felt that heart-tugging hug in return, full of unquestioning and simple love. That was the moment when the war began to lose its grip on him. That was the thread that began to draw him back into family life.

Oddly enough, though, it was a wartime acquaintance who caused the change in his business life. He received an invitation to an RAF reunion, signed by one of those worthy but tedious busybodies who customarily organize reunions, giving considerable pleasure to others and earning little gratitude for themselves.

'I don't think I'll go,' said Tom.

'You might as well,' replied Betty. 'You know you'll enjoy talking about old times –

92

and there's a play on the wireless I want to listen to.'

'It's twelve and six,' said Tom, frowning as he studied the typed form.

'Oh, Tom!'

He looked up and saw her laughing at him.

'I think you can just about afford a twelve-and-sixpenny dinner, including wine!'

He found himself laughing back at her, and realized that it was the first time they had laughed together for a long while.

He did enjoy the reunion immensely, although they didn't talk much about old times in the RAF. They were all far more concerned about trying to make a living in the hard world outside. And the pleasant thing was that most of them were not finding it too easy and didn't mind saying so. Everywhere else they had to try to put a brave face on it, but here they were among their own, like actors who all know what it is to open to an empty house on a wet Monday night in the provinces. In the lavatory Tom found himself next to a wing commander whom he had known slightly during his first posting, a tall man with a beaky nose and very blue eyes. Brent grinned at him.

'Mixed bunch, aren't we?' he said. 'I can't

think how Timmy managed to round us all up. Still, it's quite interesting to meet again and find we're all in the same boat, more or less.'

'Rowing against the tide,' said Tom. 'What do you think of all this talk of emigrating?'

'Can't say it surprises me. I've thought about it myself. But I'll have to stick it out here now. I've set up a little business.'

'Oh? What are you doing?'

'Making office furniture.'

Tom dropped the soap on the floor.

'Really?' he said. 'How very interesting.'

The wing commander laughed and picked up the soap for him.

'Glad you think so,' he said. 'No one else seems to.'

'But how did you get into it?' inquired Tom.

'Well, after I was grounded, I spent a hell of a lot of time in an office, shoving papers across a desk and polishing a chair with my bum. It struck me then that they were extremely badly designed, especially the chair. I mean, you could sit in a Spitfire all day – chuck it all about the sky – and, unless you got a bullet up your arse, you came out of it as good as you went in. But that damned office chair, it was ugly, it was clumsy, and it didn't damn well do the job it was built for. Same with the desk. So I designed new ones and set up a little factory to build 'em.'

'You own a factory?' said Tom, impressed.

'Well – more like a workshop. But I've got a few chaps, and my brother came in partnership with me, and my wife was in accounts in the WAAFs – she manages the money side... .'

'It sounds great,' said Tom.

'Well – yes...' said the wing commander. 'Of course the bureaucracy is hell, and all those damned regulations, and all the stupid buggers who keep saying, "Don't you know there's a war on?" I suppose they'll go on saying that for the next twenty years before they catch on to the fact that the bloody war's over. But we're getting the materials somehow, more or less, and we're making some good stuff, if I say so myself. I'm sure there's a market for it somewhere. The trouble is, none of us has any experience on the selling side of things.'

There was the sound of raucous applause from the dining room, and the wing commander turned toward the door.

'We'd better get back,' he said. 'Nothing on earth will stop Timmy from making his 'old comrades' speech, and I suppose we

95

ought to be there to hear it.'

Tom caught his arm.

'Just a minute,' he said. 'I think there's someone you ought to meet.'

Mr Osmund stared at Tom in amazement.

'Buy a lot of new furniture?' he said. 'You must be bloody mad! We've got a whole warehouseful of furniture now, and we can't move it.'

'We can't move it,' said Tom, 'because it's junk, and they know it's junk. They're sitting behind one rotten desk. They're not going to buy another that's no better.'

He saw an indignant look in Osmund's eyes and knew he had gone a bit far, so he hurried on.

'It's no good offering them army surplus. They know army surplus. Half of them were in the army. But if we show them a range of new, quality stuff...'

'They'll ask how much it is,' said Osmund from bitter experience, 'and say it's too expensive.'

Suddenly Tom knew what he was doing. He wasn't just a failed salesman of shoddy goods. He knew his job as he used to in the control room when he said with absolute authority, 'Find out if that's an SOS plane or a Hostile. Get on to the Observer Corps

96

at once.'

'I'm sure it's too expensive as they're making it now,' he said, 'with Brent designing it and his brother-in-law in the business and his wife doing the accounts. It's a sort of cottage industry. But if we helped them make it in bulk...'

'What's the point, when I've got a warehouseful of...'

'Oh, come on!' said Tom, exasperated. 'Anyone can buy army surplus and try to sell it. But that's the past, and soon all that will be gone anyway, and we'll be out of business. If we invest in Brent's furniture – that's the future. It's well designed, well made. It's new. Then we'll have something worth selling.'

'I like the way you say *we* invest,' said Osmund, sourly. 'How much money have you got?'

'Not a bloody penny,' said Tom. 'But if you make it, I'll sell it.'

'If I go bankrupt,' said Osmund, 'you'll be out of a job,' but he grinned as he said it.

Osmund and Brent hit it off at once – that is, if striking sparks off each other was hitting it off. Tom, being somewhat in the position of marriage broker, found himself involved in every part of the new business. Above all, he found himself in a peculiar

97

position for a somewhat impoverished employer, acting as negotiator between the two principals. Funnily enough, it was the tough East End businessman who was most easily wounded in his feelings and the artist who fought most fiercely and with most ruthless determination for his own designs in all their revolutionary purity. It seemed to be Tom's role to reconcile financial reason with artistic integrity – and he soon realized that the only argument that really counted was sales. If the public wouldn't buy the stuff, even Brent would have to modify his designs, and if they did, even Osmund would have to stop grumbling.

When it came to sales, Tom found that he had learned enough during the past months to feel surprisingly confident. He launched out upon an ambitious publicity campaign, but since Bill Osmund was agonizing over every penny spent, it had to be a remarkably economical once as well.

'I suppose,' he said tentatively to Betty, 'you wouldn't consider doing a bit of typing?'

'Oh, I couldn't come to the office,' she answered quickly. 'I must be there when the children come home from school.'

'I know, but I was thinking,' said Tom hesitantly, 'that perhaps – at home ... No, it's all right. I know you've got enough to do without that.'

'Well,' said Betty dubiously, 'perhaps if I had a typewriter here...'

'Actually,' said Tom, 'if you look in the hall, you'll see a Corona portable. I bought it today for twenty quid.'

'Tom!' said Betty. 'You're the blooming limit!'

There was something immensely satisfying about finding the whole family involved in a job that until then had been destructive of all self-esteem and that now had a feeling of adventure and pioneering, with Betty using her premarriage typing skills to address the envelopes and Lucy earnestly and precisely folding the brochures and Colin putting them in the envelopes. After the children had gone to bed, he and Betty worked on, writing letters and talking, and because Betty had spent a short time as a secretary before they were married, she came up with some remarkably useful comments on what secretaries *really* wanted from office furniture.

'There's never anywhere to put your lipstick,' she remarked, 'and nail polish remover and a bit of loose change.'

'Right,' said Tom. 'That little drawer for pencils and paperclips, we'll describe it as

99

"The Secretary's Personal Effects Drawer." Better not mention lipstick – the boss won't like it.'

'*He* might not,' said Betty, 'but it's the secretary who chooses the furniture and everything else in the office.'

'Yes,' said Tom with feeling. 'I found that out! You go to bed, darling. I'll try to draft something which pleases the secretary without tipping off the boss.'

Tom was enjoying it all so much that he really didn't want a holiday, but he received a ferocious letter from Pauli reminding him of his promise and telling him that Betty needed it even if he didn't and that he was a selfish pig. It was a sign of their new ease together that he showed the letter to Betty and they both laughed about it.

'It's no good,' said Tom, 'we'll have to manage it somehow. Otherwise Pauli will bring it up against me every time we quarrel for the next twenty years!'

'Dorset, eh?' said Osmund, unexpectedly. 'That's a good idea.'

'It is?' said Tom, startled.

'I've been thinking for some time, we haven't really moved into the west country.'

'It's not exactly a big industrial area.'

'Small businesses need new desks, and besides – there's Bristol.'

'*Bristol?*' exclaimed Tom, 'that's a bit far from...'

'You need a car.'

'I can't afford to buy a car.'

'I'll pay for it,' said Osmund. 'I've thought for some time you need one. You can drive the family down to Dorset and then take off to Bristol – maybe go on into Wales...'

'*Wales?*'

'Nice place, Wales,' said Osmund. 'I was in training near Cardiff. Quite a lot of business there. And with all this nationalization, there'll be lots of government offices. Oh yes, you'll enjoy Wales. Make a nice holiday for you.'

'Thanks,' said Tom.

'That's all right,' said Osmund.

Tom, meeting his eye, wasn't sure whether or not he had grasped the irony. One of the charms with Osmund was that one never really was.

'Oh, by the way,' said Osmund, as Tom headed for the door, 'might as well get a secondhand car. No point in shelling out for a new one.'

As the time for the holiday grew near, the children were ecstatically excited. Tom realized with guilty astonishment that they had never been on a holiday as a family before. Pauli was right, as usual. It was

101

about time. On the night before their departure, Colin collapsed into bed, lying on his back with arms flung out, exhausted with joy and excitement, but Lucy was still dancing about the house, chanting, 'We're going on holiday! We're going on holiday!'

'Now, come on, Tigs,' said Tom, endeavoring to draft an up-to-date report that would keep Osmund out of mischief until his return. 'I'm busy, and Mummy's tired out. You must be a big grown-up girl and put yourself to bed.'

Sitting at his desk (one of Brent's desks) in the distinctly overcrowded living room, he was aware of a silence and turned to see Lucy backed, motionless, in a corner.

'What's the matter, Tigs?'

'I don't want to be a big grown-up girl.'

'Why not?'

'Because then I won't be your Tigger anymore.'

Tom laughed and held out his arms.

'Come on,' he said.

She ran and scrambled up onto his knees and clung to him with all the old fervor. The papers went flying, and something thudded to the floor. Tom hoped it wasn't the inkwell but strongly suspected it was.

'You'll always be my Tigger,' he said. 'Go on, you horrible child, go to bed!'

She laughed and kissed him and went. Tom began to tidy the desk and, glancing down, was relieved to see that it wasn't the inkwell that had fallen but the calendar. He picked it up. It said July 25th.

'Oh, God!' said Tom aloud.

He wondered if Anne was thinking of him, as he was thinking of her, and whether she bitterly regretted, as he did, that they had not at least decided on that one letter a year that would have let him know if she was alive or dead. And he wondered whether that date would ever go by for her without thinking of him, as he this day thought of her.

Nine

The time that Betty went into hospital for her operation was not in the least convenient – but then, such events rarely are. It coincided with the launching of a new line in what Peter Brent called 'Executive Chairs.'

'That's a far cry,' remarked Tom, eyeing the prototype, 'from the circular wooden chair once polished by a wing commander's bum.'

'*Exactly!*' replied Brent.

'It's too expensive,' said Osmund.

'Rubbish!' said Brent, 'there isn't a managing director in the country who wouldn't love a chair like that.'

'Maybe 'e would,' said Osmund, who had taken to dropping his *H*s in anticipation of tycoonhood, 'but he's got to sell it to his board.'

He looked at Tom.

'This is going to need a special kinds of sales campaign.'

104

'It's a special chair,' shouted Brent indignantly. 'It doesn't *need* a special sales campaign.'

'Oh, you blooming idiot!' Osmund exploded. 'That's exactly why it *does* need it.'

'*Tom?*'

They both looked at him.

'Er – you're both right.'

They both exploded then, and Tom laughed.

'We've got a new brochure coming out. We'll feature the new chair on the cover. How's that?'

'Fine,' said Brent.

'Not enough,' said Osmund.

They began to speak at once. Tom put up his hand like a policeman.

'All right, I know. We have to sell it to the managing directors as a status symbol and make the board think status pays off in hard cash. I'll put something on paper, and you can both pull it to pieces, but I must get home now. Betty's going into hospital this evening.'

They both exclaimed in hasty sympathy.

'It's all right,' said Tom. 'It's nothing serious, just a small operation. But I ought to be there to drive her to the hospital.'

Betty's stay in the hospital produced an odd mixture of distress and inconvenience.

105

Even though it was only a minor routine operation, Tom felt some anxiety, and he knew that Lucy did too. Colin's chief worry seemed to centre upon whether he would get into the football team and, if he did, whether his mother would be out of the hospital in time to watch him play.

'I'm sure she'll be out in time,' said Tom, 'but I doubt if she'll be able to watch you play. She'll need to take things easy for a while.'

'Maybe she could come in a wheelchair,' said Colin hopefully.

'Heartless little brute!' said Tom.

But he knew that behind his own concern for Betty was considerable exasperation that the hospital should have arranged the thing just now, when there was an exhibition at the Olympia convention centre at which Osmund and Brent Furniture had a booth, and when he had so much work to do in planning the sales of the new chair.

It was even more annoying that the operation was delayed for a week, when they had expected it to be done next day. Tom was thankful that they'd moved to Wimbledon three years before. Lucy was now thirteen and Colin eleven. They both went to good schools where they normally stayed for lunch anyway. They had plenty of friends living nearby, so they didn't have to come home to an empty house. There was also Mrs Carter, who came in and cleaned for a couple of hours every day. She had demarcation lines, however, as firmly drawn as any shipyard worker. She did not do any shopping or cooking, and Tom didn't in the least relish the prospect of an extended diet of sausages and baked beans, or hasty shopping and flustered consultations with Lucy, which always resulted in both of them buying a loaf of bread and neither of them getting eggs.

The hospital was strict about visiting hours – just an hour and a half in the evening – so that if the children were going to visit Betty, he had to catch an early train home to pick them up and drive back through the rush-hour traffic. If he was going alone, he had to leave the office just when he felt he was beginning to catch up on his work, and get jostled about in a time-consuming journey on the Underground.

On one of these occasions he had been on the telephone all afternoon about a problem connected with the firm's booth at Olympia. It was exasperating to have to abandon the difficulty still unresolved and set out for the hospital. Betty was sitting up in bed in her best pink fluffy bedjacket.

'Sorry I'm late,' said Tom. 'I had to wait half an hour for the bloody train.'

He hadn't meant to say that, and he certainly hadn't meant to swear. He kissed her and sat down, trying to smile brightly.

'How do you feel?' he inquired.

'Oh fine! They took me down for more tests today. Goodness knows what for. I had to wait about an hour, and there was such a nice woman next to me. She said she'd been in here three times, and they still don't know what's wrong with her.'

While Betty talked with animation of events in the hospital, or Nurse This and Mrs That, Tom had trouble keeping his mind from wandering to Olympia. Perhaps they could get a revised price list printed in a hurry and simply slip it in the catalogue...

'How are things at home?' asked Betty.

'Oh – fine,' replied Tom unconvincingly. 'I never knew it took so much organization to look after three people and one house.'

'You've got your business as well,' said Betty. 'I'm sorry, darling. It *is* awkward for you. You don't have to come every day, you know.'

'Oh, nonsense!' said Tom and hoped he'd kept the irritation out of his voice. His eyes met hers, and he saw that he hadn't. She

108

smiled at him, and he smiled back.

'No, *I'm* sorry, darling,' he said. 'It's much worse for you. Why the hell can't they do the operation and get it over with? It's beastly for you hanging on day after day.'

'I'm having a nice rest,' said Betty. 'Go on, you get home. You'll get an hour's work done before supper.'

Tom got up and kissed her.

'I'll see if I can catch a doctor,' he said, 'and find out what's going on.'

He glanced at his watch as he left the small ward, thinking with the same unwilling touch of irritation that he had hoped to stop by the exhibition on the way home. As he emerged into the corridor, he saw the nurse standing at the door of her office.

'Mr Sanders,' she said, 'Dr Howard would like a word with you.'

It was extraordinarily unsettling to stand and discuss his wife's health with a perfect stranger in that tiny office, with glass walls and nowhere to sit down, and nurses bustling to and fro outside.

'You did know, Mr Sanders, that your wife had rheumatic fever as a child?'

'Yes, but it didn't leave any ill effects. I knew because ... I wondered if it was safe for her to have children.'

'She has a slight heart condition,' said the

109

doctor, 'probably as a result of that illness.'

'Oh,' said Tom blankly. 'You mean ... she can't have the operation?'

'The operation is essential,' said the doctor. 'But it does mean that there is a slight risk.'

It was an immense relief when Betty came safely through the operation. Tom had convinced himself that she would die on the operating table and, sitting alone in the chintz-covered waiting room, he had actually prayed for the first time in years. He saw the nurse approaching along the corridor – even the waiting room had glass walls – why was there never any privacy in hospitals? Her face was solemn, and he stood up, fearing the worst. She spoke solemnly, too.

'Your wife came through the operation very well, Mr Sanders,' she said.

'Thank God!' said Tom.

She did smile, then.

'She's sleeping peacefully. Now, why don't you go home and come back and see her tomorrow evening. She'll be more herself then.'

When Tom walked in next day with a large bunch of flowers and a clean nightgown, Betty was asleep. He sat down beside her, thinking that as soon as people went into the hospital, they developed a sort of anonymous look, as though they had joined another race of beings and assumed their indistinguishable characteristics. And although they longed for visits from 'outside,' they had trouble in communicating with their visitors, whom in a sense they had left behind in a world no longer theirs. But when Betty woke and he took her hand, she smiled at him and said at once, 'How did the new chair go?'

'It was a great success,' he said. 'We had it in the booth in a sort of stage spotlight, and there were a lot of inquiries about it.'

'Oh, good,' said Betty sleepily. 'You'll bring me the brochure when it comes out?'

'You'll be home long before then,' said Tom.

'Oh, yes,' replied Betty, 'so I will.'

'At least you won't have to type the envelopes this time.'

She smiled and closed her eyes again.

'How do you feel?' asked Tom anxiously.

'Oh, I'm fine. I'm just so sleepy.'

She opened her eyes again.

'Did Colin get into the team?'

'He did. Oh, I nearly forgot...'

Tom produced the letters from the children – Lucy's an elegant 'Darling Mummy, Get Well Soon,' illustrated with watercolour

111

flowers, and Colin's a drawing of himself playing football.

'Always the egotist, our Colin!' said Tom, and they both laughed.

He put the nightgown away in her locker and got a nurse to put the flowers in water, then sat holding her hand while she dozed. This time he didn't feel any impatience. He was only thankful that she had come through safe and sound.

'Will it be all right if I bring the children tomorrow?' he asked the nurse, on his way out.

'Oh, I'd leave it a bit longer, Mr Sanders. Your wife needs all the rest she can get.'

Betty died in her sleep that night.

Ten

'I'm glad Betty never knew,' said Pauli.

'Knew?' replied Tom, startled.

He was pouring her a drink and, turning, met Pauli's surprised gaze and saw that she had picked up Betty's photograph in its silver frame.

'How ill she was. Some people say everyone has a right to know, but it wouldn't have been right for Betty.'

'No,' agreed Tom. 'It wouldn't.'

He brought over Pauli's gin and tonic, and she put the photograph down and took the drink.

'Dinner won't be long,' she said.

'Mm,' said Tom. 'It smells delicious. I'm going to miss you.'

'Thanks,' said Pauli. 'I'm flattered.'

It was good to have company, Tom thought. Although it was nearly a year now since Betty died, he still wasn't used to living alone. At Pauli's insistence, both Lucy and Colin had gone to boarding school, and he knew it was right because he now travelled so much that they would have spent a great deal of time alone in the house, and none of them could face the thought of a live-in housekeeper, even if they could have found one.

'Please, Daddy,' Lucy had said, clinging to him, 'please let *me* stay and keep house for you.'

'No, Tigs,' he answered. 'Aunt Pauli is right. It wouldn't be good for you.'

But, deep in his heart, he knew that Lucy's presence, silently and pathetically grieving for the death of her mother, was a sort of reproach. He truly mourned Betty's death, yet there was guilt mixed with his sorrow, knowing that for nine years he had been unfaithful to his wife in thought and desire. Lucy's simple grief was a constant reminder of that fact.

He saw his son off on the train without too many qualms. Colin looked, it was true, suddenly very small in the somewhat over-sized grey flannel shorts and jacket that Pauli had bought him at Swan and Edgar's. But Colin, thought Tom, had always been resilient. His mother, like that ridiculous comfort-blanket called George – or was it Peter? – had already receded into the past. It was very different with Lucy. Dressed in the

114

new navy blue uniform with the huge velour hat that made her small pale face seem smaller than ever, she put her arms around him in a desperate, silent embrace and then smiled bravely up at him and climbed into Pauli's car. The pale face still bravely smiling out the back window haunted Tom for the rest of the week. Nevertheless, they both now seemed moderately happy, Lucy at the same school as Pauli's daughter, Joan, and Colin at a school near Eastbourne that seemed to be teaching him little but a new and passionate enthusiasm for rugby football, but that suited him well enough.

Tom managed to arrange all his trips during the school term so that they could spend most of the holidays together. But while they were away, he found the house in Wimbledon very desolate. He missed that pot of tea when he got home and even missed Betty's perfunctory, 'Had a good day, dear?' He took to working late at the office and having a meal out so that he just got home in time for a drink and bed. Or, if he was on a trip, he would often stay an extra night, so that he could go straight to the office in the morning. He realized that in all his life he had never before known what it was to be lonely, and that loneliness was almost like an illness, draining away his

115

courage and self-esteem. And beneath it all he felt a deep, guilty sadness that he had never been able to appreciate fully Betty's devotion, yet it was that devotion that he now missed. He looked up and saw Pauli watching him. She raised her glass.

'Cheers!' she said.

'Cheers!'

There was an awkward silence. Tom realized that there had never been an awkwardness between them before and wondered if he was losing the habit of social behavior. He bestirred himself.

'Thanks for coming, Pauli,' he said.

'Not a bit, I've enjoyed it,' she replied. 'David hates London. If it wasn't for you, I'd never get up at all.' She hesitated. 'You will look after yourself after I've gone?'

'Of course.'

'And you will eat?'

'My dear Pauli,' said Tom, 'the fridge looks like a cold-storage plant. I'll make a pig of myself every night.'

'I could stay on another couple of days.'

'Certainly not,' said Tom. 'I should think my unfortunate brother-in-law is getting fed up with cooking his own meals.'

'Do him good to be on his own,' said Pauli, and then stopped short. 'Sorry,' she said.

Tom smiled at her.

'Stop fussing,' he said. 'I'm managing all right.'

'You ought to marry again,' said Pauli.

Tom caught his breath, looked at her, took another breath to speak and then didn't, but instead got up and went to make himself another drink.

'Betty would have wanted it,' said Pauli.

Tom didn't answer, but concentrated on pouring himself a whisky.

'Tom,' said Pauli, 'did you and Betty nearly break up once?'

Tom turned to look at her, astonished.

'Toward the end of the war?' continued Pauli.

'How the hell...?' Tom stopped, alarmed. 'Did Betty tell you?'

'No!' answered Pauli quickly. 'No, of course not.'

'She didn't know,' said Tom. 'At least, I'm pretty sure she didn't.'

'You nearly broke up, and Betty didn't know?' said Pauli, frowning.

Tom finished making his drink, and spoke with his back turned.

'Well – there was a girl...'

'Ah-ha!' said Pauli.

Tom turned and glared at her.

'Not 'Ah-ha!' at all! Her father was a

117

clergyman and I...'

'You didn't want to hurt Betty and the family,' said Pauli.

Tom looked at her in silence and returned to sit down.

'But this girl – she was something very special,' said Pauli.

'Yes.' Tom hesitated. 'But we didn't ... we broke it off before ... we said good-bye, and we've never seen each other since.'

'I often wondered,' said Pauli, gazing into her glass, 'whether David met someone special while he was away.'

She glanced up at Tom and tossed back the last of her drink.

'But if he did, he'd've had her into bed in a minute, the bastard!'

She stood up.

'Can I get myself another one?'

'Yes, of course,' said Tom. And then, troubled, 'Pauli...?'

She sniffed.

'Oh damn! The dinner!'

'Was she married?' inquired Pauli suddenly.

'Who?' said Tom, tucking into the delicious *coq-au-vin*. 'Oh – no. She probably is by now. I don't know.'

'You ought to find out,' said Pauli.

'I *can't*,' replied Tom with a note of

118

despair. 'I don't know where she is. We promised each other that we wouldn't keep in touch, and we haven't.'

They ate in silence for a few minutes.

'Didn't you say her father was a clergyman?' asked Pauli.

'Yes.'

'Then you could look him up in "Jane's Fighting Clergymen" or something. You know his name, and you could go to the public library and look up his parish.'

'Oh, I know his parish,' said Tom. It was odd how readily the name came to his mind. 'He was rector of Endersby in Norfolk.'

'Well, then!' said Pauli and put her knife and fork down with an air of triumph.

She looked at Tom and saw him frowning.

'You might as well know at least if she's married.'

'Supposing she is,' said Tom. 'We'll be worse off than we were before.'

'Not quite,' said Pauli. 'If she *is* married, it's better to know it, and then you can put her out of your mind once and for all.'

Tom sat looking at his half-eaten dinner, his face expressionless.

'I've got to attend a sales conference in Norwich next week,' he said. He looked up at Pauli and grinned. 'And when I last heard, Norwich was in Norfolk.'

He picked up his knife and fork and began to eat again with relish.

'You know something, Pauli?' he said. 'You're a damn good cook!'

Endersby was a great deal further from Norwich than it looked on the map, and it took a great deal longer to drive there than Tom had reckoned, along those apparently interminable Norfolk roads, as straight as a die (whatever a die was), and as flat as a pancake. Noel Coward was right: 'Very flat, Norfolk.'

'I must be mad!' thought Tom, but he felt a tremendous excitement.

'Mares eat oats and does eat oats and little lambs eat ivy,' he sang as he drove along, and remembered how Anne's WAAFs used to sing those ridiculous words, and how she was at first exasperated by their nonsense, and then got the song on the brain herself and used to sing it to Tom, while he protested.

'Mairzy doats and dozy doats...'

'If you sing that again, I'll kiss you!'

'And little lambs idivy!'

'You asked for it!'

She shrieked and ran, and he caught her. Tom was smiling at the memory of the laughter and kisses as he saw the signpost to

Endersby.

There was no difficulty in finding the church. Its tower rose up above the small village like a cathedral. Tom parked the car outside the fine lych gate and walked up the path. The churchyard looked badly overgrown. Hard to get help, he supposed – and the rector must be getting on in years. Tom saw a woman tending a grave not far away. She wore a clumsy skirt and a shapeless woollen jacket, so he presumed she was a local inhabitant, and he turned toward her. He was just about to speak when he heard the clank of a heavy door and saw a clergyman coming out of the vestry. He paused and locked the door behind him. He wore a cassock and was about thirty years old.

'Must be the curate,' thought Tom as the young man approached.

'Good afternoon,' he said. 'Did you want to see the church?'

'Well, actually,' replied Tom, 'I – er – er – I wanted to see the rector.'

'I'm the rector,' said the young man, smiling pleasantly. 'How can I help you?'

Tom was conscious of opening and shutting his mouth like a fish.

'Er – I – er – you're not Mr Hawthorne?'

'No. My name's John Reading.'

'Oh.'

Tom was so unprepared for this that he knew he was behaving like an idiot. He said feebly, 'Mr Hawthorne isn't here?'

'No,' said Mr Reading. 'I'm afraid...'

He looked toward the churchyard, and Tom, following his gaze, saw a comparatively new, large gravestone set flat in the grass, though unlike some of the others, it had the grass trimmed around it.

'You mean...?' said Tom, and walked to look down at it.

IN MEMORY OF GEORGE HAWTHORNE,
RECTOR OF ENDERSBY 1928–1948.
BORN SEPTEMBER 13th, 1895.
DIED JULY 4th, 1948.
ALSO OF CLARA, BELOVED WIFE OF THE
ABOVE, BORN JUNE 12th, 1900,
DIED FEBRUARY 3rd, 1943.
'God is faithful.'

Tom heard the young rector approaching and turned to look at him, dismayed.

'I'm so sorry,' said Mr Reading, concern on his face. 'Were you related?'

'No,' answered Tom.

He was aware of the woman surreptitiously listening as she tended the grave nearby.

'I knew his daughter, Anne Hawthorne,'

122

said Tom. 'Does she still live here?'

He was amazed when the young man frowned thoughtfully. How could a clergyman in a small village not know the former rector's daughter?

'I don't believe...' he said. 'The old rectory's turned into flats now, and people rather come and go, but...'

'You don't live in the rectory?'

'Oh no, no!' exclaimed the young rector, almost shocked at the very notion. 'I have a new house, just outside the village. Much smaller, you know, much more manageable. But Miss Hawthorne – I don't think...'

He became aware of the woman, who had now given up all pretense of not listening and had straightened up, watering can in hand.

'Mrs Wilton! Do you know Miss Hawthorne?'

'Oh *yes*,' she said. 'I knew her well!'

Tom felt a sudden sharp pang, a blow to the heart.

'*Knew* her?'

'She moved away, you know,' said Mrs Wilton in her strong Norfolk accent. 'Yes, she moved away after the old rector died.'

'Ah,' said Mr Reading, 'that would be during the interregnum.'

'The what?' said Tom.

'The time between rectors,' said Mr Reading helpfully. 'Mr Hawthorne died very suddenly...'

'That he did!' interrupted Mrs Wilton, with just a touch of ghoulish pleasure. 'Poor Miss Hawthorne, she come into his study one morning, and there he was – dead in his chair!'

'Oh, no!' said Tom. 'What a shock for her.'

'So it was, sir,' agreed Mrs Wilton. 'She just found him there, and...'

Mr Reading intervened. It occurred to Tom that the rector didn't like Mrs Wilton and that she didn't like him.

'That was why there was some delay,' he said, 'in finding a new incumbent. Most younger ministers prefer to work in industrial areas. But I felt that a country living was a real challenge.' A note of cheeriness came into his voice as he spoke of himself. 'I look after three parishes here now. I live in Endersby, of course, and this is the mother church, but we're not quite the close-knit community we used to be – eh, Mrs Wilton?'

'We are *not*, Rector,' she replied, with considerable emphasis and a resentful glance.

Tom spoke hastily. 'But Miss Hawthorne – you said she moved away. Do you know where?'

124

'Oh – I *don't*, sir!' cried Mrs Wilton with an air of enormous willingness to oblige. 'You see, my husband, he went into hospital just after the old rector died, and I went to stay with my sister, over to Norwich, so's to be near, and what with complications and one thing and another – I must've been gone nigh on three months, and when I came back – well, my husband passed on soon after that – and the rectory was all shut up, and Miss Hawthorne had gone away.'

'I suppose,' said Tom with a sense of hopelessness, 'she didn't leave a forwarding address?'

'She did, sir!' responded Mrs Wilton, triumphantly.

'Ah,' said Mr Reading, obviously hoping that this signaled the end of the business. 'That *is* good news.'

'Yes,' continued Mrs Wilton, 'she left it with Mrs Ainsworth – she used to clean for the old rector while Miss Hawthorne was away in the WAAFs. I remember Fanny Ainsworth saying to me, "It's only on a scrap of paper. I hope I don't lose it."'

Tom hoped so too.

'Where does she live?' he asked.

'That cottage there, at the end of the street.'

Tom followed Mrs Wilton's nod of the

head and saw a small, square flint cottage. He turned toward it with a sense of excitement.

'That is, she *used* to,' added Mrs Wilton, 'but she went to live with her son last year. In Australia.'

'And – you don't know *her* address?'

'Oh, no,' replied Mrs Wilton, faintly surprised. 'She's in Australia.'

It might have been the moon. Anne could be in Australia, thought Tom. She could be anywhere. It was as though in leaving Endersby she had made the final break with him.

'I must know if you're still alive.'

'Don't worry – I won't be.'

'Well,' said the young rector, finally and with determination, 'I'm so sorry we weren't able to help you. Er – if you would like to look at the church – we have to keep it locked, I'm afraid – vandals, you know – but Mrs Wilton has the key.'

There were a great many garish leaflets in the porch, but inside the church was unchanged in all its lofty austerity. It was odd to stand in that place where Anne had spent so much of her childhood and youth. Tom wondered which pew she had worshiped in for so long. He remembered her speaking of 'the rectory pew,' and how he

126

had teased her, asking if it was one of those box pews with high walls so that the rector's family could go to sleep in the sermons.

'No,' said Anne, 'but it has a high hassock because we go to church more often than anyone else and spend more time on our knees.'

Tom saw a pew with a hassock bigger than any of the others and thought, 'That's the rectory pew.' He imagined Anne kneeling there in her WAAF uniform, and it was almost as though he could see her in the dim light beneath the stained glass window, like a ghost. He became aware of Mrs Wilton in the doorway.

'Knew Miss Hawthorne well, did you?' she inquired.

'Oh – no – I met her in the war and promised if I was ever anywhere near, to visit her and her father.'

He added the last three words for the sake of Anne's reputation, but he doubted if Mrs Wilton was deceived.

'It's really a shame you should come all this way and be disappointed,' she said.

Tom left her locking the church with a big iron key and was aware that she was watching him as he walked through the churchyard, following the overgrown path that he knew from Anne led to the small picket gate

127

into the garden of the rectory.

He had that haunted feeling again as he looked up at the big bare house, because Anne had told him about it, and now he was there, but she was gone, as though she had died and lingered now only as a ghost. Ugly boards by the front door read: 'Flat 1. Flat 2. Flat 3.' He thought of ringing one of the bells, but what could he say? 'I've come to see a girl I knew in the war, but she's not here any longer.' Still, he found that he could not resist walking around to the back of the house. Perhaps the back door would be open and he could go into the kitchen and glimpse some fragments of her life there, touching, like a pilgrim, the things that she had touched.

Another ugly board by the back door read: 'Flats 4–6.'

'God! It must be like a bloody rabbit warren in there,' thought Tom.

He hesitated, wondering whether to ring one of the bells, still aware of that absurd feeling that Anne was there somewhere and that if he could only get inside, he would find her waiting for him.

'You won't find no one in there!'

Tom turned and saw an old gardener clipping the hedge that once had divided the lawn from the vegetable garden. He had a

128

strong Norfolk accent.

'Out all day, they are, or only come at weekends,' he added.

Tom walked toward him.

'I was looking for Miss Hawthorne,' he said.

The old man's face brightened.

'Miss Hawthorne? You mean, Miss Anne. Very nice young lady she was. Very friendly. More like her mother than the old gentleman.'

'You knew her!' said Tom.

It seemed a stupid question, but the old man beamed a toothless grin.

'Been gardener here for thirty years. Knowed Miss Anne since she was a little 'un.'

'You don't know,' said Tom, 'where she went when the rector died?'

'No, I don't know that,' said the old gardener. 'She never told me that. "I'll 'ave to get a job, Alf," she said, "when I leave the university, I ain't got no money."'

'But you don't know where?'

'She never said. Sent me a Christmas card once, but I don't know where from.'

'No,' said Tom. A sudden thought came to him. 'The university?' he exclaimed. 'She went to the university?'

''At's right,' said Alf. 'When she come

129

back from the war, she said, "I'm going to the university, Alf," she said, "on what they call one o' they ex-service grants.'"

'Do you know which university?' asked Tom.

Alf looked at him, his faded blue eyes surprised at such ignorance.

'Well,' he said, 'it'd be either Oxford or Cambridge, 'ouldn't it? I mean, when they say university, that's what it is, en't it? Oxford or Cambridge.'

Eleven

Tom drove back from Norfolk so exhilarated at having at least a clue to Anne's whereabouts that it was only when he got home to Wimbledon and sat down with a corned beef sandwich and a cup of coffee that he realized how difficult it was to follow up. Not having been to college himself, he had no idea to what extent they kept in touch with their old students. He knew it would be a women's college, but as a matter of fact, he didn't even know the names of the women's colleges at Oxford and Cambridge – even supposing that Alf was right, and Anne had gone to one or the other. He very soon gave up the notion of writing a letter to the heads of all those colleges, saying, 'Dear Madam, I fell in love with one of your students, Miss Anne Hawthorne, some time ago, and would like to know where she is now.' Even when he decided to write to Anne, addressed to the college and marked 'Please forward,' he didn't find the letter an easy one to write.

'Darling Anne...' No, he could hardly say, 'Darling Anne,' and then tell her that his wife was dead. He started again.

'Dear Anne, I know you will be sorry to hear that my dear wife...' No, that sounded – somehow –Victorian. But if he said, 'Dear Anne, Betty is dead...'

In the end he just wrote: 'My dear Anne, I wanted you to know that the situation has changed and that there is nothing to stop us meeting now. I would very much like to be in touch again. You can reach me at the above address,' and he signed it, 'Ever yours, Tom.'

He asked his secretary to find out the names and addresses of the colleges, on the pretext that he wanted to know because of Lucy. There were more than he had

131

thought, and he was too impatient to send it to each college in turn and wait for a reply, so he typed out a copy of the letter for all of them, addressing it, with a qualm, on Betty's Corona, and marking each one, 'Please forward.' He tried not to think about the possibility that Anne had gone neither to Oxford nor Cambridge and that he would have to repeat this performance with every university in the country. In the end he needn't have worried. He had put his address on the back, and the other colleges all returned his envelope marked 'Not known.' But from Newnham College, Cambridge, it had been re-addressed to The Rectory, Endersby, Norfolk, and returned with a Norfolk postmark and a scrawled inscription, 'Address not known. Return to Sender.'

'There must be some way of finding her,' said Pauli.

'If there is, I can't think of it,' answered Tom.

Pauli had come up to London for some early Christmas shopping. Tom, signing letters at his desk, glanced up at her.

'The stupid thing is,' he said, 'that until I couldn't find her, I wasn't even sure that I wanted to. And now...'

He read a letter through and corrected it and spoke without looking up.

'Maybe that means I don't really care, after all.'

'Don't you?' said Pauli.

Tom looked up at her as she sat perched on the windowsill above Holborn.

'Yes,' he said, 'I do.'

He signed his name and closed the letter file and pushed his chair back.

'It's like discovering you're hungry,' he said. 'Once you've thought of it, you can't think of anything else.' He smiled ruefully. 'I really thought I'd forgotten her and now I can't think of anything else.'

'Oh, Tom,' said Pauli.

She left her perch on the windowsill and came to sit down opposite him.

'We said we'd make it impossible to find each other,' said Tom. 'We've done too good a job.'

'I can't believe,' said Pauli, 'that there isn't someone who knows where she is.'

'There are plenty of people, I should imagine,' replied Tom irritably, 'including her husband, for all I know. Unfortunately I don't know *them*!'

'What about the RAF reunion you went to?'

'That was quite a different lot, from my

133

first posting.'

'And there was no one from the station where you met who might have kept up with her?'

Instantaneously pictures flashed across Tom's mind. There was Mavis with that painted enamel complexion saying, 'Get orff yer arse!' Bender saying, 'Cheerio, Tom.' Bender saying, 'Coming to the station dance tonight, Anne?'

'Bender!' he exclaimed. 'Pauli, you're a genius! Come on, I'll take you out to a bang-up fish supper at Wheeler's.'

He was halfway out of his office while Pauli was still gathering up her parcels.

'Did you say you were going on a bender?' she demanded.

Tom turned and grinned at her.

'Something like that,' he said.

It was easy to arrange a trip to Birmingham. Their sales representative there wasn't doing a very good job, and if he couldn't improve, he'd have to go. Tom, remembering how hopeless he himself had been when he began, wasn't looking forward to the interview, and in the end, it was worse than he expected because the man seemed perfectly satisfied with his performance. When someone who is doing a lousy job thinks that he is doing perfectly well, there is not much hope for improvement.

'I'll have to sack him,' said Tom when he got back to the cold comfort of his hotel room, and he said it aloud. He was getting into a bad habit of talking to himself.

Rather surprisingly, Tom had Bender's home address. In the course of that splendidly disastrous station dance, Mavis Bender, rather late in the evening and after her fifth whisky, developed a slightly maudlin affection for Tom while they were dancing.

'I want to tell you something,' she had said, leaning perilously backward so as to gaze into his eyes, 'you're a nice fellow.'

'Thank you,' replied Tom, strengthening his grip so that she would not fall flat on the floor with him on top of her. 'That's very nice of you, Mavis.'

'No!' she said with a touch of aggression. 'I didn't say it to be nice. I speak as I find. You're a nice chap. Bendy likes you, too.'

'Oh. I'm glad.'

'There's not many people Bendy and me both likes. People take him for a ride, you know.'

'I don't think...'

'Yes, they *do*!' said Mavis, glaring at him. 'When I first met him he told me he hadn't a penny to his name. Those bloody trustees

135

of his was making away with it all. There's not many people I'd tell this to.'

'Er – no,' said Tom, wishing she wouldn't tell him.

'I said, "You'd better get yourself a lawyer," I said. "There's one that come in here for a brandy every evening, regular as clockwork."'

'Good God!' thought Tom. 'She *is* a barmaid!'

'He's related to a lord, you know,' said Mavis.

'The lawyer?'

'No, Bendy. That's where the money come from, but the trustees said it was all tied up. "Well, they can bloody untie it," I said, "and when they've done it, *I'll* look after it." I 'ave, too. 'E's all right now, but I have to keep an eye on him, or he'd give it all away. There's not many people you can trust.'

The music came to an end, but Mavis still held Tom, bringing her face close to his.

'That's why I like you. I'll give you our address, so's you can come and see us after the war.'

'Oh – yes,' answered Tom. 'That'd be – great. Er – shall we sit down?'

'No!' said Mavis, aggressive again. 'You give me something to write on, and I'll jot it down now, while I remember.'

Tom managed to draw her to the edge of the dance floor, and she wrote it in the back of his diary while Anne, standing nearby, watched with immense amusement.

There was an anxious moment when Tom, searching for the diary, was afraid that it might have been thrown away in the move to Wimbledon, but he came upon it at last in a battered old leather suitcase, with his uniform and his service identity card and all the other faded paraphernalia, so small and limp and shabby, to represent the war that had seized all their lives in a huge and iron grip. *The Air Force Diary, 1944*, with wings and crown on the cover and pictures of aircraft inside. On the back page written in pencil in a large and wandering hand, he read, 'Hugo and Mavis Bender, 24 Hazel Avenue, Solihull.'

Sitting there in his hotel room in Birmingham, Tom knew that he should have written ahead, but he had been afraid to. They might have moved or died – he was beginning to have a morbid feeling that everyone involved in his search dropped dead just before he reached them – and he knew that the Benders were his last faint link with Anne. If he couldn't find them, then he would have to admit that he had lost her forever. He got out the telephone book from

137

the bedside cupboard and turned the pages over. When he found it almost at once, he could hardly believe it. 'Bender, H. A., Sqdrn. Ldr., 24 Hazel Avenue, Solihull.'

It was Bender who answered the telephone, and he seemed to have become rather deaf. But when he grasped who Tom was, he was clearly delighted.

'I say! Jolly good to hear from you! Splendid! Splendid!'

'I wondered if I could come and see you,' said Tom.

'Splendid! Splendid! How long are you staying?'

'Well – only tonight. I thought, perhaps, if you're not doing anything else – I might come over this evening.'

'Ah.'

Clearly there was some difficulty.

'Yes,' said Bender. 'We'd – um – like to ask you to come and have a bite, but...'

'Oh no!' said Tom hastily. 'I meant, after dinner.'

'Ah!' The relief was unmistakable. 'Splendid. It's just that...' he dropped his voice slightly. 'We usually have high tea, you know, and I'm not sure that...'

'No, no!' cried Tom. 'I was thinking, perhaps I could come along for a cup of coffee, or...'

'Fine,' said Bender. 'Splendid! Look forward to seeing you.'

It was Bender who welcomed him into the detached suburban house, Bender unfamiliar in tweeds, but otherwise much the same.

'Come in, come in!' he cried. 'How about a snifter?'

A pungent aroma inside the house indicated the nature of their 'high tea,' and the next minute Mavis, emerging from the kitchen, confirmed it.

'Sorry about the smell, dear,' she said when she had greeted Tom warmly. 'Bender always cooks the tea, and of course he would have to get kippers this evening. *And* he only got two so we couldn't ask you to join us.'

'That's quite all right,' said Tom.

It was startling to find that Mavis looked just as incongruous in a suburb of Birmingham as she had in an operational RAF station. She had the same white enamel complexion with the unconvincingly high spots of color on each cheek, which somehow made her look like a miniature of Queen Elizabeth the First in old age, the same plucked eyebrows penciled in brown, and mascara in great gouts on her eyelashes. And, instead of the mauve crepe dress, she wore a tight pink tweed skirt, a lacy woollen jumper, and a large number of bracelets that jingled with every movement as she led the way into the drawing room.

'Great to see you again, Tom!' said Bender, and headed for the drinks table. 'What will it be?'

'Now then, Bendy,' said Mavis sharply. 'Tom doesn't want a drink. He'd much rather have coffee. I've put it all ready. You go and make it.'

'Righty-ho,' said Bender.

'I have to keep an eye on him,' said Mavis when he was barely through the door, 'or he starts lifting the elbow. Not enough to do, you know, now they've pensioned him off at last.'

She hitched up her tight skirt with both hands, easing it over her bottom, and sat down.

'Now, come on dear,' she said, 'tell me about yourself. Where are you living now?'

The coffee was highly genteel, all flowered china and silver and doilies, and Bender kept being sent back to the kitchen for things he'd forgotten, so that it seemed hours before Tom was at last settled with coffee, cream, and sugar and a biscuit he didn't want, and managed to ask casually, 'Do you ever see anything of the old gang?'

'No, not really,' answered Bender.

'They were rather a common lot, weren't they?' Mavis interposed. 'Present company excepted.'

That seemed to put a stopper on talk about old times – Tom could hardly say, 'Anne wasn't common!' to get it going again. His mind working frantically, he managed, 'Oh, I don't know – some of them weren't too bad. Er – Parker-Jones and – and' (what the hell was his name?) 'Craven, and – Anne Hawthorne. Remember her?'

'Anne Hawthorne,' said Bender vaguely. 'Now, let me think – oh yes. Nice girl. Rather mousy. I remember Mavis saying, "You'd know she was the daughter of a clergyman. No hanky-panky with her."'

'Not like that redhead!' said Mavis, and gave him a sharp look through those mascara'd bead curtains.

'Do you know where she is now?' asked Tom.

'The little redhead?' asked Bender, startled, and got another sharp look from Mavis.

'No, no!' cried Tom hastily. 'Anne Hawthorne.'

'Haven't a clue, old boy,' said Bender. 'Why?'

'I just – wondered,' said Tom, and thought he got a shrewd look from Mavis.

'Tell you who I *did* see the other day,' said

Bender. 'Jimmy Pratt.'

'Good Lord!' said Tom. 'Don't tell me he survived the war?'

'Without a scratch, old boy. You'll never guess what he's doing now – flying for BOAC. Those passengers don't know what a chance they're taking. Wonder if young Freddy Pierce came through all right. If so, he's probably flying with Air France. Remember his French girlfriend? Ooh-la-la!'

Suddenly Tom found himself caught up in one of those long-winded and pointless conversations about half-remembered people and events. As it petered out, he saw Mavis glance at the clock, and desperation made him abandon all finesse.

'Talking of Anne Hawthorne...' he said.

'Who?'

Bender was definitely getting deaf. Tom raised his voice.

'Anne Hawthorne. You don't know how I could get in touch with her? Do you suppose it's any good writing to the Air Ministry?'

'No idea, old boy. I suppose they'd probably have an address for her. As long as she's at the same place she was during the war. They could look it up in records... .'

'It wouldn't be the same address,' said

142

Tom. 'She's moved.'

'Ah, well, then ... how about a snifter, old boy, before you go?'

'No, thank you,' said Tom, standing up. 'I've got a long drive tomorrow. I'd better be off.'

Mavis and Bender didn't try to stop him. They stood up too. Perhaps after high tea they went to bed early. In another moment, thought Tom, he'd get the bum's rush and be outside the door. He stood his ground.

'You can't think of any friends of hers at the wing who might know where she is?'

'Who?' said Bender.

'Anne Hawthorne,' said Tom with grim determination.

'No-o,' replied Bender. 'Can't think of anyone.'

'Oh.'

Tom gave up and turned toward the door.

'What about that tall, beaky WAAF officer?' said Bender.

'Which one?' demanded Tom, turning back.

'They were friends, weren't they? What was her name? Parnell? Or was it Morrison?'

'I've no idea,' said Tom. 'I don't remember her at all. Do you know where she lives?'

'Not a clue, old boy,' said Bender.

Mavis said good-bye to Tom in the drawing room, and as he waited for Bender to get his coat and hat from the hall closet, Tom heard the chink of bottle on glass. Maybe Mavis was having a quick snifter herself so as not to put temptation in Bender's way. He remembered how he and Anne had laughed at the Benders at that dance, and felt a deep misery at the thought that they would never laugh at them together again.

'Good-bye, Ben,' he said. 'It's been great to see you again – and Mavis too.'

'What a girl, eh?' said Bender, proudly beaming. 'God! That was a lucky day for me when I walked into the Rose and Crown!'

Tom realized that he meant it and that it might even be true. He wished that Anne was there to know it with him. Bender opened the front door, and he prepared to go out.

''Ere!'

It was Mavis, in the doorway to the drawing room, and sure enough, she had a glass of whisky in her hand.

'If I wanted to get in touch with Anne Hawthorne, you know what I'd do?'

'What?' demanded Tom.

He really didn't care any more what they thought. He just wanted to find Anne.

'I'd put an ad in the personal column,' said

144

Mavis.

'My dear,' said Bender, 'he doesn't particularly want to find Anne Hawthorne.'

'Don't 'e?' asked Mavis, and knocked back her whisky.

Tom drove back to London the next day with a sense of desperate impatience. He felt as though he had been given the one sure way of finding Anne and he couldn't wait to put it into action. That it should come through Bender and Mavis, who were there when he and Anne first met, seemed like a sign and so did the fact that this time he had no doubt at all about the words he wanted to say: 'ANNE. The situation has changed. Now we can meet and hurt no one. Remember the primroses. I love you always. TOM.' He wrote it out in his own hand because he didn't want to use Betty's Corona typewriter for this, and he left it at the office of *The Times* himself. Clergymen always read *The Times*, and Anne's father was a clergyman. She would certainly read *The Times*.

Tom's unreasoning sense of hope and excitement continued. He bought *The Times* every day and, since they now spent Christmas with Pauli, and since his sister and brother-in-law bought the *Daily Telegraph* and knew that he did too, it wasn't easy to

145

explain his new need to purchase *The Times*. Somehow this was so much a personal matter between himself and Anne that he didn't want to share it even with Pauli. He hastily invented an item of business news that he was looking out for and then found himself in trouble when David asked him exactly what it was.

'Oh – nothing very interesting,' said Tom.

'Ho-ho! a commercial secret, eh?' said David, who as a Regular Army officer sometimes seemed to feel it essential to adopt the air of a simple, bluff soldier.

'Something like that,' replied Tom.

He didn't really expect Anne to communicate with him in the personal column. He had given a box number, and it was more likely that she would write. But he was certainly taking no chances in case she might choose to answer by the same means as he had used and he might miss it. If she thought that Betty was still living – or, worse still, if she herself was married – she might send the kind of answer intended to shut him out of her life again, but at least, thought Tom, he would know that she *was* alive.

That Christmas was a comparatively cheerful one. Lucy and Colin seemed to have recovered to some extent from their

146

mother's death, and Pauli and David, although they argued a good deal, did so in a high-spirited way as though they needed such jarring to keep the spark of marriage alight. It must have seemed as though Tom took part in all the festivities, the games and presents and gathering of local people for drinks and parties, but in fact he hardly felt that he was there at all. He could think of nothing but this need, which had become an obsession, to find Anne. And when Christmas had come and gone and the only message in the paper was his own, he felt a desperate urgency to get home. He had not dared to give his address or telephone number in case one of his friends or family spotted it, but if Anne had written to the box number, *The Times* would have forwarded it.

The drive back to Wimbledon through the returning Christmas traffic seemed interminable. He was aware of Lucy and Colin wrangling irritatingly throughout the journey, and of other drivers, with the baby's crib on the roof and packages piled over the back window, impeding his progress, but he could think of nothing but whether there would be a letter from Anne, and whether it would say – 'Yes! Do let us meet!'

When they arrived and he picked up the

147

letters from the mat, he couldn't wait a second longer to leaf through them. Lucy staggered in with a bag full of presents. Tom glanced at her and tossed the pile of envelopes on to the hall table.

'Nothing interesting,' he said. 'Mostly late Christmas cards.'

'Were you expecting something?' inquired Lucy.

Suddenly she sounded like her mother.

'No,' said Tom. 'Why?' And before she could answer, he added, 'I'd better get Colin's bike off the roof rack.'

As he wrestled with the knots that David had so enthusiastically tied, Tom reminded himself that the mail was always completely dislocated during the Christmas season. His message had only been in the paper for two weeks. There was plenty of time for Anne to see it and to reply, and he was absolutely certain that she would.

Lucy and Colin were still on holiday, but fortunately, much as it annoyed him in the normal way of life, they slept late. Tom was trained to rise early, not only by his service life, but even more by Osmund.

'Get in the office early,' Osmund used to say. 'Set a good example.'

What this really meant was that he used to help his father in Petticoat Lane Market and

148

still never slept after six A.M. The fact that he left after lunch and didn't return was never mentioned. Still, Tom was glad now of that habit of early rising, and as soon as he heard the rattle of the letterbox, he tiptoed downstairs. As he picked up the letters, listening for any sound from upstairs, he remembered Anne saying how awful it would have been for him to sneak downstairs for that one precious letter a year so as to get there before Betty. She was right, he thought. It would have been awful. But now Betty was dead, and he had loved her to the end in their own way, which had nothing to do with the way he loved Anne, and *now* ... Please God, he thought, let there be a letter! And each day he was disappointed.

When the letter did come at last, it came by the second post, and he was completely unprepared for it. He came home late from the office and heard Colin playing records upstairs. Lucy emerged from the kitchen.

'Hullo, Dad. There's a letter for you from *The Times*.'

'Oh?'

He was proud of his command of his countenance.

'Perhaps they want you to write for them,' said Lucy.

149

'I doubt it,' said Tom.

He picked up the letter with *The Times* imprint on the envelope, and the two or three bills beneath it, and took them away into his study. Thank God, he thought, that he had a study in the Wimbledon house and didn't have to read it in the bosom of his family.

He tore open *The Times* envelope and took out the envelope enclosed in it. The handwriting subconsciously surprised him. It was – somehow – childish. He realized that he didn't know Anne's handwriting. They had never written to each other. The envelope was Basildon Bond, and the postmark was West Kensington. He lingered over these facts, reluctant to open the letter in case it should say what he didn't want to know. He tore it open at last.

'Dear Tom,' said the letter. 'I am not your Anne, but I love to pick primroses. Please let us meet. You won't be disappointed. Annie.'

Tom dropped the letter on the desk with an exclamation of disgust. He felt humiliated and cheapened and ridiculous, and, what was worse, he felt as though he had humiliated Anne as well and cheapened their love for each other.

'Was it anything interesting?' asked Lucy.

He glanced around and saw her in the

doorway.

'The letter from *The Times*?'

'Oh – no,' Tom answered. 'It was just an advertisement.'

He tore the letter into tiny pieces and put them in the waste paper basket.

When Lucy and Colin had gone to bed, Tom got out the old leather suitcase again. He meant to put the 1944 diary away and because his intention was to bury it deep so that he would never think of it again he moved his uniform aside. As he put the diary with the others he saw an envelope that he didn't remember and, without consciously meaning to, he took it out. Inside was a shabby yellow folder of photographs. He took them out and recognized them as snapshots that Anne had taken with her box camera. She had given him the prints she thought he would like to have – Bender outside the Ops. Room, the wing commander, Tom's car and driver – shuffling through them, Tom stopped short. It was a photograph of Anne outside the pub called The Reed Thatcher. He remembered that she had taken a photograph of him and then, at his insistence, given the camera to him.

'Cheese!' he had said, and she had laughed.

151

There she was in her WAAF uniform outside The Reed Thatcher, still laughing, still loving him.

'Oh, God!' said Tom. 'I must forget her!'

He put the snapshot in the folder and the folder in the envelope and stuffed it at the very bottom of the case.

'Anne,' said Phyllis, 'can I borrow your *Daily Telegraph*?'

'Er – yes,' answered Anne. 'I haven't finished the crossword yet.'

'Oh, that's all right,' said Phyllis, coming to pick it up. 'That's what I wanted to look at.'

'The crossword? I thought you didn't like crosswords.'

'No, but Gareth does.'

'I see,' said Anne, smiling.

Gareth was a superior young man from the accounts department who invited Phyllis to concerts occasionally because his mother worried that he never went out with girls.

'I thought I'd just say, "What did you get for one across? Oh, *I* put down – something else."'

She studied the paper.

'Three across – Corgi. I'll remember that. Corgi. Thanks.'

She returned the paper.

'Oh, really, Phyllis!' said Anne, laughing.

'Well,' said Phyllis, 'you can't tell them the truth all the time. It's not good for 'em.'

She picked up her gloves and umbrella and the capacious patent leather handbag in which, Anne knew, she would have the little silk dress that she would change into that evening. Phyllis was always smartly dressed, in a curiously impersonal way, rather as though a window dresser had done it. She turned at the door of the flat and called back.

'Are you going to the office today?'

'No,' replied Anne, 'it's my reading day.'

She was still in her dressing gown and poured herself another cup of coffee. She became aware that Phyllis had not gone out but had returned a few steps into the room and was standing looking at her.

'Something wrong?' Anne inquired.

'You going out this evening?'

'No?' answered Anne, puzzled.

'So you'll be at home all day and alone this evening?'

'Don't worry,' said Anne, laughing. 'I've got plenty of work to do.'

'I *do* worry about you,' said Phyllis. 'You don't have any social life.'

'Of course I do. I go out with Ted now and

then.'

'Oh – Ted!' said Phyllis. 'You might as well go out with your brother.'

'I haven't got a brother,' said Anne. 'If I had, I would.'

She saw Phyllis's long anxious face beneath the jaunty green beret, and added, 'I have a social life. When I'm not doing anything else, I sit in a pub and hold hands.'

'*What?*'

'Nothing,' said Anne. 'I was just joking.'

'Oh.'

'Go on, you'll be late for work.'

'Lumme!' said Phyllis, 'so I will. Cheerio!'

'Cheerio,' said Anne.

'Cheerio,' indeed! What a ridiculous expression. She returned to the *Daily Telegraph* crossword.

Twelve

Colin went back to school first.

'I don't think that's fair,' he said. 'Girls ought to go back sooner.'

'Why?' demanded Lucy rashly.

'Because they're more stupid. They need longer to learn everything.'

'Ooh, you little...'

It was an enjoyable wrangle, and it lasted all the way to Eastbourne.

'What are you going to do when you leave school, Tigs?' asked Tom on the way home.

'Look after you,' replied Lucy promptly.

Tom glanced at her and smiled.

'I'd like that,' he said, 'but I think it would be a good idea if you went to the university as well.'

The telephone was ringing as Tom opened the front door, and he hurried to answer it, irrationally, since Anne didn't have his telephone number.

'Bender here.'

'Who? Oh – yes – Bender!'

It turned out that Bender was coming up for an RFC reunion dinner, and Mavis had suggested that since he had a couple of hours to spare, he should call on Tom. Perhaps, thought Tom, she didn't want him to have too many snifters in the bar of the RAF Club beforehand.

'I don't think you've met my daughter, Lucy,' said Tom.

'No,' said Bender, shaking hands, 'but I remember your father talking about you. He said you'd just got your first pony, and that you fell off three times and enjoyed every minute of it.'

'Enjoyed it?' said Lucy. 'I loathed it!'

'You did?' said Tom, startled. 'We always thought you loved it.'

'Ugh!' said Lucy. 'I loathed it. I was terrified. I gave up riding as soon as I could. I just didn't want anyone to know why.'

'I never realized you were so secretive,' said Tom. Lucy smiled at him and then turned to Bender.

'I'm just going to get Dad's supper,' she said. 'Would you like to...'

'No, thanks,' said Bender. 'Off to a reunion dinner. Just stopped in to say there

156

was something I remembered after your father called on us at Solihull.'

'Oh,' said Tom.

He hoped that Lucy might leave to start preparing supper, but she didn't.

'Craven!' said Bender.

'What?'

'That chap you were talking about,' said Bender. 'It was Raven.'

'Oh,' said Tom.

Bender beamed at him.

'Kept niggling at me mind,' he said. 'It wasn't Craven, I thought. What was it? Then I remembered.'

'Raven,' said Tom.

'Exactly!' cried Bender triumphantly. 'Raven. Stockbroker.'

'Ah,' said Tom. 'You're right.'

He didn't give a damn what the fellow's name was. He couldn't even remember him.

'Right,' he said. 'What will you have? A whisky?'

'Thanks, old man,' said Bender. 'Mustn't stay too long, or I shall miss the soup.' He paused and added, 'Terrible soup always at these dinners, but makes a change from Heinz Tomato. Mavis won't have anything else.'

'Ah,' said Tom, and went to pour him a drink.

'By the way,' said Bender, 'I knew there was something else I meant to tell you. That girl you were trying to find – Anne Hawthorne.'

Tom observed with dismay that Lucy was still there, perched on the arm of a chair near the door.

'Mavis said you might put an ad in the personal column of *The Times*!' remarked Bender, laughing heartily.

'Yes,' answered Tom, attempting an unsuccessful answering laugh, 'so she did.'

'Well, old boy,' continued Bender, 'I tell you what – I know where she is.'

Tom remained quite still, his hand on the whisky bottle.

'Oh, really?' he said, without turning around.

'Absolutely, old boy. I was talking it over with Mavis, after you left. Her father was a clergyman, I said, and I remember I told her that we used to spend our holidays on the Norfolk Broads. "We live in Norfolk, near Thorpe!" she said. Extraordinary thing, it came to me just like that when I was talking to Mavis. "You'd better tell Tom when you next see him," she said.'

'Yes,' said Tom, and finished pouring the whisky. 'I believe she did live in Norfolk, but she moved away after her father died. Still, thanks very much for mentioning it. Soda?'

Tom was glad that Lucy was going out to a small party at a friend's house that evening. Before Bender was into his second snifter, she had gone out to change and returned to tell Tom that his supper was in the oven, and to say a polite good-bye to Bender. Tom wondered what she made of him. With her hair in a pony tail and her tight-waisted full-skirted dress, and ankle-strap shoes, she looked like a charming little girl pretending to be grown up.

When at last Bender left – he would certainly miss the soup – Tom was thankful to sit down to his solitary meal and then to spread out his papers and documents in the study and get to work. At least, that's what he meant to do, but ... Damn Bender, anyway! Stupid, thick-headed clown. When he heard Lucy's key in the front door, Tom was sitting staring straight ahead, thinking of nothing. He hastily put on his spectacles and pulled the latest sales figures toward him. When he heard Lucy open the study door, he spoke without looking around.

'Hullo, Tigs. Have a good time?'

'All right,' she answered. 'Listened to some records and drank some coffee. Was your supper all right?'

'Very good.' He looked around and smiled

159

at her. 'I'm going to miss your cooking.'

She came into the room.

'I hate to leave you alone.'

'I'll be fine,' said Tom. 'You'll be back for half-term before we know it.'

He swung the chair around – Brent's Executive Chair – took his glasses off, and held out his arms.

'Good night, Tigs. You'd better get to bed.'

'What about you?' asked Lucy.

'I'm not tired. I think I'll do a bit more work.'

She came to kiss him.

'Would you like some coffee?'

'No, thanks,' said Tom. 'I've had some. Off you go.'

She turned toward the door, and he thought he'd gotten away with it, so it was all the more shock when she turned back and said, 'Dad, who's Anne Hawthorne?'

'Oh...' said Tom, '... she ... Mummy and I knew her during the war.'

'Why do you want to find her?' asked Lucy.

'I don't,' said Tom quickly. 'That is...'

'Squadron Leader Bender said...'

'Yes. Well – when I was in Birmingham, I called on him and his wife and – we were talking about old times, and I thought he might – that is, I asked him if he remem-

160

bered her.'

'And he did.'

'Yes.'

'And you asked him if he knew where she lived.'

'Yes. That is...'

'Where does she live?' asked Lucy.

'If I knew where she lived,' said Tom violently, 'I wouldn't be...'

'Trying to find her,' finished Lucy.

There was a silence. Lucy sat down.

'Were you in love with her?' she asked at last.

'No, of course not!' said Tom.

There was a longer silence this time. He must say something. He couldn't just make some dismissive remark and turn his chair back to the desk, leaving between them that half-discovered, unexplained secret. And yet, thought Tom, how could he describe in a few minutes that mixture of love and loyalty, of passion and faithfulness, and describe it to his daughter, who was still suffering from the wounding loss of her mother, and his wife, whose memory his story must seem to slight. He decided that the kindest thing was to lie – as he had already lied – and to say, 'It's not in the least important, Tigs. Go to bed.' He looked up and met Lucy's eyes, loving and candid.

'I'm sorry, Tigs,' he said. 'That wasn't true. I did love her once, but we ended it before anyone got hurt. Mummy never knew anything about it.'

Lucy's eyes left his. She looked down at the carpet, frowning. Tom felt as though in telling her, he was telling Betty too, and he was aware of a desperate need for her to understand.

'These things happen in wartime,' he said. 'Working together in the control room all night – being responsible for the safety of your planes – keeping in touch with them, plotting them and then – counting them in, knowing which ones are missing, which ones you've nursed safely home. It's the sort of thing you share together, as though you're in a different world for a time, with a life and death responsibility and a pride in sharing it.'

He found he was explaining it to himself as well, looking back at those two uneasy lovers as though from another world.

'And then you step outside,' he said, 'in the early morning when it's still dark and everything's cold and fresh, and you're so tired that you feel – disembodied – and you stand and talk and look up at the stars, and you're not conscious of each other as flesh and blood. You feel each other's essence,

162

and you never forget it.'

He glanced up at Lucy.

'That's the kind of love it was for both of us – something quite separate from ordinary life.'

He waited for a moment. Lucy sat motionless, still staring at the carpet.

'Anyway,' said Tom, 'it's all over now, and I've no idea where she is. Go to bed, Tigs.'

Lucy looked up at him.

'But, Daddy, that's awful!' she said. 'Why, she might be living just around the corner, longing to hear from you!'

Tom was so relieved that he actually laughed.

'I doubt it!' he said. 'I'm not as sentimental as you are. I think she's probably living somewhere near Norwich, married, with four children.'

'Why Norwich?' inquired Lucy.

'Well, her father was a rector in Norfolk, and after he died she...'

'She came to London,' finished Lucy.

Tom stared at her, and his mouth fell open.

'She could be in the phone book,' said Lucy.

'Oh, come on!' said Tom, laughing, but his laughter slowly died away.

Lucy jumped up.

'I'll get it!' she said, halfway to the door. They kept the books beside the telephone in the hall.

'I'm sure,' said Tom, 'that she won't be – I mean...'

What he really meant was that it wouldn't be right. It would be too easy. In a way it would almost be ridiculous to think that he had been desperately searching for her, and all the time...

Lucy returned with the telephone book. She looked eager and excited, enjoying the romantic adventure. Tom took the book and put on his glasses. As he turned the pages, looking for 'Hawthorne,' he was trying to remember her initials.

'Anne...' he said. 'She had three first names – I remember laughing about it. I confessed to Percival, and hers were – annoyingly respectable.' He sat still, with the book on his knees. 'Anne Elizabeth Rushmore.' He was amazed again to find how swiftly it sprang into his mind. 'Rushmore was her mother's family name.' He began to turn the pages again. 'Dean – Drew.' He closed the book and looked up at Lucy. 'You never did know your alphabet! It should be E to K.'

'Oh, yes,' agreed Lucy, 'so it should.'

She seized the book from him, laughing,

164

and ran to fetch the other one from the hall. Tom had become caught up in her enthusiasm. Suddenly it was all a game, an adventure.

'Hurry up, Tigs,' he called.

Lucy returned with the right book, and Tom seized it and turned over the pages.

'Hawkins,' he said, 'Hawthorne, A...' He paused. 'A.E.R. Hawthorne.'

Tom caught his breath. It was like turning a corner and coming face to face with her and having no words to say. He looked at Lucy.

'You'd better ring her,' said Lucy.

Tom glanced at the clock on the mantelpiece.

'It's too late now.'

'No, it isn't!' cried Lucy. 'No one goes to bed before eleven. Write the number down.'

'Er...'

Tom didn't understand why he felt such reluctance, and he tried to conceal it as he copied the number down on a scratch pad.

'Better put the address, too,' urged Lucy.

Tom did so. Flat 3b, and an address in South Kensington. 'Thank God it's not West Kensington!' thought Tom, remembering the crazy woman who'd written in answer to his advertisement. Lucy took the book back.

'Go on, Daddy,' she said. 'Ring her.'

She went toward the door.

'I'm going to bed,' she said. 'Tell me what happens in the morning.'

'Of course,' answered Tom. And then, 'Thanks, Tig.'

She smiled at him.

'Good luck!' she said and shut the door behind her.

What a sensitive little creature she was, thought Tom. She knew, whether it was good news or bad, he wouldn't want to talk about it that night. He took a deep breath and dialed the number. As it rang, he found himself clearing his throat nervously.

A very efficient-sounding woman's voice repeated the number.

Tom was sure it was Anne, but it seemed better to say cautiously, 'Could I – er – may I speak to Miss Anne Hawthorne, please?'

'Speaking,' she said. 'Who is this?'

'It's – it's Tom.' He paused. It seemed quite ludicrous, but after all, she might by now know other men called Tom, so he added, 'Tom Sanders.'

There was a long silence.

'Are you there?' asked Tom.

'Yes.'

There was no doubt now in his mind that it was Anne, but her voice had a curious

166

quality of suspended animation.

'I've been trying to find you,' he said.

'Oh. Have you?'

Tom hadn't considered how to say it, but his next words came very naturally.

'My wife – Betty – she's dead, you know.'

There was some warmth then in her voice as she answered, 'Oh, I'm so sorry!'

'Thank you,' said Tom.

There was another pause. Tom felt like a clockwork toy slowly running down.

'How are you?' he asked.

'Oh – fine,' said Anne. And then, after a pause, 'How are you?'

'Fine,' said Tom.

He felt that what little impulsion he had was finally ended and that he had nothing more to say. They were two strangers marooned at each end of the telephone.

'Um,' said Anne, and he thought that she, too, was having to wind herself up to speak, 'Um – are you – um – in London?'

'Yes. Yes, we live in Wimbledon.'

'We?'

'Well – the children – Lucy and Colin...'

'Oh, yes. Of course. How are they?'

'Fine,' said Tom.

It was another dead end, but at least she had made that slight move toward him, and it was with a tiny, reviving glow of eagerness

167

that he said, 'I was wondering – perhaps we could meet for a drink or a meal?'

'Oh, yes, I'd like to.'

Her voice had a little life in it now.

'How about tomorrow night?' asked Tom, his eagerness growing.

'I can't tomorrow. I'm – I'm going to the theatre.'

Cancel it, thought Tom. Damn it, cancel it! But he just said, 'Oh.'

'Er – I'm free on Thursday,' said Anne.

'Oh – right,' said Tom and then, as he glanced at his engagement pad, 'Oh. No. I'm taking Lucy back to school. And – well, then I have to go to Birmingham on business.'

'Yes, I see.'

There seemed almost to be a moment when, from sheer hopeless inertia, they would break this tenuous thread between them and break it forever. Tom made a final effort.

'Perhaps one day next week?'

'Oh, yes!' He caught the note of desperation in her voice too. 'How about – Monday?'

'Well – Tuesday would be better for me.'

'Tuesday.' There was just a second of hesitation before she continued. 'Yes. That would be – fine.'

'Right!' said Tom with a briskness that also came from desperation. 'I'll probably be coming straight from the office – and there's quite a good little restaurant not far from you. Guiseppi's. Do you...?'

'Yes, I've seen it,' said Anne.

'Right. Let's meet there. Shall we say – seven-thirty?'

'Yes,' said Anne. 'Seven-thirty. Good-bye.'

'Good-bye,' said Tom.

Thirteen

'Oh, don't say it's raining!' exclaimed Anne. 'Now I'll never get a taxi.'

'I thought Ted usually picked you up here,' said Phyllis, taking off her pale pink head scarf and shaking it delicately between finger and thumb.

'It isn't Ted. It's – someone else. Someone I met during the war.'

'Lumme!' said Phyllis. 'A secret romance, eh?'

'No, of course not,' said Anne irritably.

'No offence, I'm sure,' said Phyllis, wounded.

169

'I'm sorry, Phyllis,' said Anne. 'It's just that...'

'That's all right, dear,' replied Phyllis, always easygoing. 'I didn't mean to pry. Something special, is he?'

'I'm not sure,' said Anne.

Her feelings in the days since Tom telephoned had been an extraordinary mixture of excitement and dismay. It was wonderful that Tom had come back to her again – even if it was only by telephone. And – Betty was dead – they were free to be happy together. So why did she feel uneasy? It was partly the memory of that awkward telephone conversation, but also – there was something else – something that lurked at the back of her mind, creeping indefinite and unidentified upon her joy.

Still, all her thoughts were centred upon the meeting, and she lived again that other, secret life, even while she was going to the office, reading manuscripts, interviewing authors, criticizing illustrations. When she went to the theatre she was aware of the fact that Tom was in Wimbledon and that she could walk out of the play and hail a taxi and go to him. (She had looked him up in the telephone book, and there was only one T. P. Sanders, so she knew his address.) And during the weekend she knew he was in

Birmingham. Odd, and subtly satisfying, to know that much at least, after so long of not knowing where in the whole world he might be.

Anne booked a hair appointment on Tuesday afternoon. It was not her usual hairdresser, but a younger one, who said, 'Would you like a fair rinse? You could do with a little bit of colour.'

'Oh – yes, why not?' said Anne, and then watched in some alarm as her brown hair took on the unfamiliar golden lights.

Did it look like peroxide?

'Ooh, you've had your hair done!' said Phyllis as she walked in. 'Lovely!'

How absurd, thought Anne, to 'have her hair done' for Tom, and she wasn't exactly encouraged to know that Phyllis approved of it! Then, the dress she wore – it was her favourite. It had a full skirt and showed her small waist, but was it just a little too ... too...? But then, she thought, after all, Guiseppi's was quite an elegant little restaurant. It was not a pub! And then, suddenly, she knew what was wrong. Tom should have rung her when the pubs were open. He should have said, 'I am here! Come!' and she would have left everything and gone to him.

''Bye,' said Phyllis. 'Have a good time.'

171

'Thanks,' said Anne.

There is always something theatrical about entering a candlelit restaurant. Anne found herself gracefully yielding her fur coat to the attendant at the door at the very moment she became aware of Tom, sitting at a table set for two. She walked toward him, and he rose, then the waiter was there moving the table out so that she could sit next to Tom.

'Anne.'

'Hullo, Tom.'

As she sat down – 'Would the signorina care for a drink?'

'Oh – yes. A glass of sherry, please.'

She looked toward Tom, but the waiter was still at her elbow.

'Dry or sweet?'

'Oh – medium, please.'

'*Va bene*, signorina.'

The waiter busied himself, emptying Tom's ashtray and giving each of them a huge, tasselled menu. When at last he went away, they looked at each other and smiled uneasily.

'You look just the same,' said Tom. 'Except that – your hair's different.'

'Is it?' said Anne. 'You...'

'I've put on weight,' said Tom.

'Well...'

She saw the grey eyes and the round, humorous face, and began to smile, but the waiter was there again.

'Sherry, signorina?'

He put the glass down with an almost caressing gesture. He was one of those waiters who conduct a small flirtation with the lady diner, usurping the place of her partner.

'Thank you,' said Anne.

The waiter, with a flourish, produced a pad and pencil and looked at them expectantly.

'We're – not quite ready yet,' said Tom.

The waiter raised a deprecating hand and retired. Anne and Tom looked at each other like children who hadn't done their homework. Because she was beginning to feel she hated it...

'This is a nice place,' said Anne.

'It's convenient if you're going to the Albert Hall,' said Tom.

'Oh, I didn't know you were musical.'

'I'm not, really, but...'

Was he going to say his wife was? thought Anne.

'Lucy is,' finished Tom.

Anne nodded and smiled.

'And I know she likes riding,' she said.

'Well – so we thought. Poor little kid, she

was only three, and my parents piled her up on the local farmer's pony. She was terrified, but they were so proud of her that she tried to pretend she was enjoying it. You never know what children are thinking.'

'No,' said Anne.

The waiter was hovering again. Tom opened his menu.

'Well,' he said, 'perhaps we'd better...'

When they were finishing their prawn cocktails, Anne asked brightly, 'What are you doing now?'

'I'm in business,' answered Tom. 'Osmund and Brent Office Equipment.'

'That's not your own firm?'

'No, I'm sales director.'

'Do you enjoy it?'

'Yes, I do rather,' replied Tom, his tone defensive. 'Have you got a job?'

'Yes. I work for an educational publisher.'

'As a secretary?'

'No,' said Anne. 'I'm one of the editors.' She didn't mean it to be crushing, but she knew that was how it sounded.

'I do beg your pardon!' said Tom ironically.

She laughed uneasily.

'That's quite all right. I just – prepare the books for the printers and liaise with the illustrators and so on.'

174

'Educational,' said Tom. 'Sounds impressive. Of course you have a degree, haven't you? You went to Cambridge.'

'How did you know that?' demanded Anne, startled. 'That was after...'

Tom took a breath to answer, but the waiter was there, sharp as mustard, to remove the dishes and refill their wine glasses.

'How are the children?' asked Anne when at last they had achieved the main course, saying yes or no to innumerable vegetables and assuring the waiter that they had absolutely everything they needed.

'They're hardly children now,' said Tom. 'They both went to boarding school when Betty died, and Lucy's in the fifth form this year.'

'How odd,' said Anne reflectively.

'What?'

'All this time I've been thinking of them as children – Colin quite a baby, and Lucy – Lucy a little girl on a pony.'

'How have you thought of me?' asked Tom.

Anne answered quickly, almost angrily. 'I've tried not to think of you!'

Tom took a breath, but there was suddenly a small dark man, Guiseppi presumably, beside their table.

'Is everything all right, sir?' he inquired.

175

'Yes, thank you,' said Tom. 'Everything is fine.'

He should have added, 'to coin a phrase' thought Anne.

They hardly spoke during the rest of the meal. It was like a dreadful travesty of their parting in the pub in Sussex, with chattering fellow diners all about them, while they were held apart in their own emotional impasse. As they drank their coffee, Anne said suddenly, 'I've never seen you out of uniform before!'

Tom looked at her, startled.

'No,' he said, 'I suppose not.'

'We even went to dances in uniform,' said Anne.

'Did we?'

'Very odd,' said Anne, looking back, amused, 'dancing in a collar and a tie and flat shoes.'

'Yes,' replied Tom. 'I suppose so. Come to think of it, I don't believe I ever saw *you* out of uniform, either.'

'The whole thing was so phony, wasn't it?' said Anne.

She saw the look on his face and hastened to explain.

'I mean,' she said, 'the whole war thing – going about in romantic uniforms, saying we were saving the world from tyranny.'

176

'Weren't we?' asked Tom.

'Well,' said Anne bitterly, 'if we were, we didn't make it, did we? Look at it now. Poland. Hungary. Czechoslovakia. The labour camps in Russia.'

'At least we closed Belsen and Buchenwald,' said Tom.

'Did we know about those at the time?' said Anne.

'I'm not sure.'

Anne knew that in attacking the heroic image of the war they had fought together she was attacking also the romantic love they had shared, but somehow she couldn't stop.

'We just had a lot of propaganda about old Nasty, and wicked Goebbels and fat Goering with all his medals,' she said, 'and we thought that when it was all over everyone would be free. We hadn't a clue, really. Just wore grey lisle stockings, and...'

'Speak for yourself!' said Tom.

They both laughed, but uneasily, and then their eyes met and they stopped laughing, and suddenly the evening was over.

'Well,' said Anne, feeling under the table for her handbag, 'I suppose...'

'Yes,' said Tom. 'Waiter!'

Outside the flat, Tom took the key from Anne and put it in the latch. He opened the

177

door and gave the key back to her.

'Well...' he said.

'Thank you for a lovely evening,' said Anne.

Tom hesitated just a moment too long before leaning forward to kiss her. Anne turned her face away, and he kissed her on the cheek.

'Good night,' she said, and went inside and shut the door.

Phyllis had washed her hair and was putting it up in curlers, looking in the mirror of her beauty case while keeping one attentive eye on the television set.

'Oops!' she said, as Anne came in. She started up, endeavouring to gather up case and curlers.

She saw that Anne was alone and sank back.

'That's all right,' she said. 'I thought you might be bringing him back with you. Did you have a good time?'

Anne's misery had been growing on her all the evening like a sickness, and now it overcame her. Her one thought was to reach the seclusion of her bedroom. She walked toward it and just managed to get there. Once inside, she sank slowly down on to the floor, leaning against the door, and the grief that overwhelmed her was shameless, irresistible, the grief of all those years of irrational, unacknowledged hope.

'Naught's had, all's spent,
When our desire is got without content.'

Fourteen

As he travelled back to Wimbledon in the empty, ill-lit Underground train, Tom reflected that he had not felt so miscrably inadequate since those first days at Osmund's. And somehow he felt that it was all Anne's fault. Why did she have to get herself up like that, in an expensive fur coat and that dress with the full skirt, cut low over the bosom? It was not that their relationship had been asexual, quite the contrary! He remembered those lovely long legs as she leaned over the plotting table, and they were in grey silk, not lisle – but what he had always loved about her was the demure look, with a twinkle of amusement behind the primness. And then, her hair – surely it had not been that colour before? Against his will, he heard Betty's voice.

'Blonde? Oh, Tom, she dyes it!'

'She does?'

Tom let himself into the empty house. Why, he thought, did she have to say all those derogatory things about the war? It was as though, in tossing the war aside, she trampled on their love, which was so much a part of the war, or rather, in which the war had played so large a part.

It was true they had never seen each other out of uniform, and uniform, as he had bitterly learned shielded him from reality, from being just a poorly educated salesman. Perhaps she hadn't meant it, but she had made it clear that her job was better than his, or at least that it was a job that depended on a better education. For the first time she had made him aware of the difference in class between them, which war, the greatest of all levellers, had made irrelevant.

Tom, undressing in the big empty bedroom in the big empty house, saw the love as wasted love and the long years of cherishing it as wasted years.

It was a relief to him to be back in the office next day doing work he knew and did well. Moreover, because of his trip to Birmingham, there was some urgency, and even drama, in the day's work. Tom had noticed before that there was, after all, a resemblance between war and business, the same need to take charge in emergencies, the same responsibilities that had to be shouldered, the same necessity to explain his actions to his superiors.

'You're sure Perkins has to go?' inquired Osmund.

'Certain,' replied Tom. 'His sales figures are way down, and the trouble is, he's perfectly satisfied with them, which means they're not going to improve.'

'Well,' said Osmund, 'you're the boss.'

'I'm not,' said Tom, 'but it's very good of you to say so!'

They both laughed. That was really why Tom enjoyed the job so much. Even if it was, with a little luck, turning into a million-pound business, he and Osmund and Peter Brent had remained like slightly overweight and distinctly overage Musketeers, taking on the world. But for the moment, he had the comparatively small but complicated business of replacing the Birmingham sales manager. As he walked back along the corridor to his office, he was already thinking about a replacement and planning the letters that had to be written.

'Come in, Megan,' he said to his secretary.

He was in the middle of dictating when the telephone rang.

'Blast!' he said, but because he was nearer,

181

he picked up the receiver himself.

'Yes?' he answered curtly, endeavouring to hold that next tricky sentence in his mind. 'Sanders here.'

'It's Anne.'

'Oh. Yes.' He managed a forced warmth. 'Hello.'

'I got your business number from the telephone book. I hope you don't mind.'

'Not at all,' said Tom, but with a little, wry smile.

'I just wanted to thank you for the dinner last night,' Anne said.

'Glad you enjoyed it,' said Tom. 'I did too.'

Even as he said the words, he could hardly believe it. Were he and Anne really talking to each other in that ridiculous way? Why weren't they saying, 'God! wasn't last night hell? I don't know what was the matter with us!'

'I just wondered,' said Anne, 'whether you could come and have dinner here one evening. I mean, at the flat.'

'Yes, I'd like to,' said Tom. 'Er – when were you...'

He gestured to Megan, who passed his engagement calendar across the desk.

When they had arranged a date and time, Anne put the telephone down and sat quite still. Last night's tears had left her purged

182

and, in a funny way, refreshed. It was as though the past had been washed away and a path to the future left clear. She could even begin to smile at that awful encounter in the restaurant and to think that she and Tom would laugh about it together when they met again. It had been crazy to meet in public for the first time after so long, but perhaps it had been just as well to do it in that way and to get it over with. Now they could meet again, no longer as former lovers, but as two people who liked each other and wanted to get to know each other once more.

She must plan the dinner, she thought. It would be the very first time she had prepared a meal for him, and the prospect made her unreasonably, disproportionately excited, as people are, she thought, who are in love. She pulled the shopping pad toward her and found a note on it in Phyllis's handwriting: 'Hope you're feeling better. Keep your spirits up. P.' Anne smiled. She was immensely grateful to Phyllis for leaving her alone the night before and for setting off for work at her usual time that morning instead of hovering solicitiously about. Still smiling, Anne tore the note off and began to think pleasurably about the menu for the dinner. Chicken casserole with mushrooms.

183

She had never had cooking lessons, and all her real experience had been in war-time or just afterward at the rectory, when food was rationed. But since coming to London she had occasionally entertained at the flat, and chicken casserole was her best and most reliable dish. And to start with – no – she thought, remembering the waiter busying about. It would be a simple home meal, with one dish followed by a dessert, and she and Tom would sit and look at each other across the table and learn to be at ease together again.

But when the day arrived and Anne was setting the table, euphoria was invaded by nervousness. Phyllis emerged from her bedroom in a silk dress and short fur coat and sat down to put on her lipstick. It was one of her irritating little habits to complete her toilette in the sitting room, but Anne was glad of it now. She felt that she needed company.

'You don't have to hurry out,' she said. 'Stay and have a drink with us.'

'Not much!' replied Phyllis. 'I know when I'm not wanted. Two's company, after all.'

'He's – just an old friend,' said Anne uneasily.

She straightened a fork and glanced up and met Phyllis's eye.

'Thanks for not asking me about the other night,' she said.

'Oh well, live and let live, that's my motto. When you share a flat, it's not a good idea to live in each other's pockets. Everyone needs a bit of privacy.'

'Yes,' said Anne. 'Still, it was a bit of a performance.'

Phyllis was correcting the edge of her lipstick, making faces in her hand mirror.

'You said you knew him in the war,' she said in muffled tones.

'Yes.'

'How long did you know him?'

'Not long, really,' said Anne, and felt surprise as she said it.

Phyllis put her lipstick away and spoke in a matter-of-fact tone.

'But you never forgot him, eh?'

'I meant to,' said Anne, 'but...'

'Meant to?' said Phyllis. 'Why?'

Anne was sorry that she had not simply thanked Phyllis for her reticence and vanished into the kitchen, but it was too late now.

'He was married,' she said.

Phyllis closed her handbag with a snap.

'Oh, my dear,' she said, 'don't get involved with a married man, whatever you do. I know it's none of my business, but still – I mean, I've known it so often. All that "my wife doesn't understand me" stuff, and then, when he's had enough – well, I mean, where does it leave *you*?'

'Honestly, Phyllis, it's not like that,' said Anne, caught between indignation and amusement.

'That's what they all say, dear,' said Phyllis wisely.

'No – when he rang me – he said his wife's dead.'

'Oh well, then, that's all right,' said Phyllis and, as an afterthought, 'if it's true.'

'Oh, Phyllis!' cried Anne, laughing, and then the doorbell rang.

Phyllis started up.

'There he is. I'll be off.'

'Oh no!' cried Anne, 'stay and have a drink.' And then, with a note of panic, 'Don't go!'

She got a funny look from Phyllis as she went toward the door but was relieved to see her sit down again.

Anne should have been pleased to see Tom holding a bunch of flowers, but she wasn't. It was a sort of – stranger's thing to do. She should have laughed and said, 'Oh, Tom, I'd much rather have primroses!' but she didn't.

'Oh – thank you,' she said. 'Lovely.'

Tom began to take off his overcoat.

'Oh – let me...' said Anne.

'No, it's quite all right.'

They had a brief struggle for the overcoat, and then Tom put it on one of the pegs by the front door and turned into the room. Anne thought he looked disconcerted when he saw Phyllis.

Anne's flat was not in the least what Tom had expected. It was bare and impersonal, as though it had been furnished by a decorator and no one had yet moved in.

'You haven't met Phyllis Carr,' said Anne. 'We share the flat. This is Tom Sanders.'

'Pleased to meet you,' said Phyllis. She had a slight cockney accent.

'How do you do?' said Tom.

Anne put the flowers down.

'A glass of sherry, Phyllis?' she asked.

'Oh – yes, all right. Don't mind if I do.'

My God, she's staying, thought Tom.

'You're an old friend of Anne's, are you?' asked Phyllis.

'Er – yes.'

How much did she know?

'I always say, the old friends are the best friends,' said Phyllis.

Tom could think of no answer to that one, so he just smiled politely, while Anne brought Phyllis her glass of sherry.

'Whisky for you, Tom?' asked Anne.

'No, thanks,' he answered, without particularly caring what he drank. 'I think I'll have a sherry too.'

'Oh,' said Anne, clearly taken aback. 'Right.'

Tom, glancing toward the drinks on the side table, saw an unopened bottle of whisky. Oh damn! he thought. She'd bought a bottle specially. Well, it was too late now. He suddenly felt stifled. This was a woman's flat, where whisky was especially bought when a gentleman caller came. Anne brought his sherry and one for herself.

'Cheers!' said Phyllis. 'I mustn't stay long. I'm meeting some friends at the Chicken Inn. We were going to see *Separate Tables*, but we couldn't get in.'

'What a pity,' said Tom feebly.

'Are you fond of the theatre?' inquired Phyllis.

'Er – yes – quite,' said Tom.

'Anne's mad about it, aren't you, Anne?' said Phyllis. 'I think she's seen every play on in London.'

Tom had a horrible fleeting notion that Phyllis was trying to sell Anne to him like an army surplus desk.

'Excuse me,' said Anne and vanished, presumably into the kitchen.

Tom looked around the room, registering

the dining area and the table laid for two with the unlit candles on it. He looked back and saw Phyllis eyeing him thoughtfully.

'This is a pleasant flat,' he said. 'Have you been here long?'

'Ooh, I don't know. I must be – what? – three years. Doesn't time fly?'

'Yes,' said Tom. 'It does.'

Phyllis tossed off her glass and stood up.

'Well,' she said, 'Sorry to drink and run. Anne!'

Anne returned, looking flustered.

'Oh, must you go?' she asked.

'Simply must, my dear,' said Phyllis. 'The girls'll skin me if I'm late.'

Tom stood up and she shook hands with him.

'Bye-bye,' she said. 'Very nice to meet you.'

'Yes, good-bye,' said Tom. 'Have a nice evening.'

'Thanks very much,' said Phyllis, heading for the door. 'Cheerio.'

As the door slammed behind her, Tom was surprised to find himself wishing that she had stayed a bit longer.

'What does she do?' he asked as he sat down again.

'She's a buyer.'

'What does she buy?'

Anne looked at him, surprised.

'Clothes. You might not think it, but she goes to Paris quite a lot. She doesn't buy models but chooses models to copy. She's quite an expert in her field.'

'She's not married?' asked Tom.

'No, she's a sort of – perennial bachelor girl. Always going out with "the girls."'

'And does she ever go out with the fellows?' asked Tom.

'Sometimes, but never anything serious.'

'How about you?' said Tom. 'Do you ever go out with the fellows?'

'Never you mind!' said Anne.

They both laughed, but it wasn't quite an easy laugh.

'Another glass of sherry?' asked Anne.

'Thanks.'

Tom felt he needed it. On the whole, he was sorry he hadn't asked for whisky, after all.

'Guess who I saw the other day?' he said as she went to pour it.

She glanced around inquiringly.

'Bender. You remember him?'

'Squadron Leader Bender. Yes, of course. And his wife Mavis. She had dyed black hair.'

'Was it dyed?' said Tom. 'Yes, I suppose it was.'

'I'll get a vase,' said Anne.

For heaven's sake, thought Tom irritably, why did the girl have to keep jumping up and down? Anne called back from the kitchen.

'Are you hungry?'

'Starving.'

'I haven't done anything fancy,' said Anne. 'Just a casserole.'

'Good,' said Tom.

He began to feel more comfortable, and the dinner certainly smelled good.

'What's Bender doing now?' Anne asked, returning with the vase.

'He's retired. He and Mavis live in Solihull.'

'Really?' said Anne. 'How extraordinary. I can't imagine Bender as a civilian.'

'We're civilians,' said Tom, looking up at her.

'That's true,' said Anne, smiling down at him.

She went to put the vase on a table across the room.

'I wonder how that man is,' she said, 'whose wife was so keen that he should get promotion.'

'Who was that?' inquired Tom idly.

'You remember him,' said Anne. 'Sandy. His wife wanted scrambled egg on his cap.

191

We used to joke about it.'

Tom drank his sherry. He felt pleasantly tired and relaxed.

'You and he?' he asked.

Anne turned toward him and paused.

'Yes,' she said. And then, 'I'll get the casserole.'

She went toward the kitchen, speaking over her shoulder.

'Would you like to open that bottle of wine?'

Tom looked at the bottle of red wine and decided that it wasn't too bad, though the corkscrew was the usual inefficient woman's one. As he struggled with it, he heard a clatter of dishes from the kitchen and glanced toward it, thinking that it was good to have a woman cooking for him again. He put the opened bottle on the table, then saw the unlighted candles and made a slight grimace. There was something forced about dinner for two with lighted candles. Oh well, he thought, what the hell! Let's see if we can make a go of it this time. He took out his lighter and, as he finished lighting the candles, he saw Anne standing in the doorway, the casserole in her hands. Tom went to turn the light off and smiled at her.

'Thank you,' she said.

'I don't even know if you're a good cook,'

said Tom.

Anne laughed.

'You'll just have to find out, won't you?'

She put the dish down on the table, and he came to hold her chair for her. As she sat down, she smiled up at him, and suddenly, in that soft light, she looked as he remembered her.

'Do you remember,' said Anne, as he went to sit opposite her, 'those bacon sandwiches we had in the control room in the early morning on D-Day?'

'And Pratt came in and saw the whole table covered with gliders and said, "What's going on?"'

'Yes!' said Anne, laughing. 'I really think that was the best meal I ever had in my life.'

'I'll bet this is better,' said Tom.

Anne passed a plate to him across the table.

'Well,' she said, with the confident glow of the successful cook, 'it's only chicken and mushroom casserole.'

'Oh!' said Tom.

He took the plate and put it down in front of him, staring at it.

Anne looked at him, startled.

'What's the matter?'

'I'm terribly sorry,' said Tom after a pause. 'That's the one thing I can't eat.'

'What? What is?'

'Mushrooms,' said Tom. 'That's the one thing I can't eat. I'm allergic to them.'

'I'm sorry,' said Anne dazedly. 'I – didn't know.'

'There's no reason why you should,' said Tom.

As soon as he had finished speaking, he thought, *There must have been a better way to say that*, but then it was too late. She was not his wife. She was not his mistress. They were almost strangers.

After that, the evening could only go downhill, which it did with sullen determination. She made him an omelette to replace the casserole, but since she wouldn't allow him into the kitchen, saying it was too untidy, he sat alone, interminably it seemed, watching the candles burn down, until at last she emerged with a piece of yellow-brown washrag.

She struggled with a chicken bone congealed in fat while he ate. The vegetables by this time were pallid and chilly.

'Oh dear,' said Anne, 'I suppose I really ought to heat them.'

'Don't bother,' said Tom.

Anne looked at him.

'No,' she said, 'I don't think I will.'

And she blew out the candles.

Fifteen

'I think I shall move to the country,' said Tom.

'To Norfolk?' inquired Pauli, innocently replanting an uprooted bulb.

'No,' said Tom. 'Not Norfolk.'

It was one of those spring days that only England knows – the air fresh and that first warmth in the sun that gives promise of a summer that may never come. Tom had been to a sales conference at Bournemouth ('cheaper out of season!' Bill Osmund had said when they arranged it). It made a good excuse to come and spend a weekend with Pauli in Hampshire.

She and David had bought the house during the war, so as to have a permanent family home while he was overseas. It was just a shabby little cottage in 1940, but over the years Pauli had built on and built up, until now, though still called Twyford Cottage, it was an attractive rambling house with an equally rambling garden.

'I might buy a house near here,' said Tom. 'The kids would like it.'

'What about your job?' asked Pauli.

She was weeding the flowerbed while Tom sat on the garden bench and drank a cup of coffee.

'I might sell out my shares and pack it in. I'm getting fed up anyway,' answered Tom. 'Peter Brent's got an idea for another new line.'

'Oh.'

'He reckons that all the children who were born after the war will be growing up and needing rooms of their own where they can do their homework and "pursue their hobbies." So he's designed a whole lot of desks and folding beds and so on.'

'Sounds like a good idea,' said Pauli.

'Yes – maybe – but it's got to be sold, and someone's got to sell the idea first, and it won't be easy.'

'You'll love doing it,' said Pauli. 'You know you will. That's why you like the job. It's a challenge.'

'I think I'm getting a bit tired of challenges,' said Tom.

Pauli eyed him balefully while she struggled with a recalcitrant piece of ground elder.

'What're you going to do, then? Sit and

twiddle your thumbs?'

'Do you mean now?' asked Tom. 'Do you want some help with that?'

'Is that an offer?' inquired Pauli.

'Not really.'

'That's what I thought,' she said. 'If you buy a house in the country, *you'll* be grubbing about in the flowerbeds and *I'll* be sitting luxuriating in a cup of coffee.' And then, in the same breath, 'Why not Norfolk?'

Taken by surprise, Tom could only gasp. Pauli sat back on her heels.

'I take it you didn't find her in Norfolk – or that you did, and she was married.'

'I didn't find her then. I found her later, and she isn't married.'

'She isn't?' said Pauli, and thought it over. 'Has she become fat?'

'No.'

Pauli waited.

'We don't seem to have anything to say to each other.'

'Oh, Tom! I'm so sorry. Still, I suppose the first time, after so long, is bound to be a bit sticky.'

'We tried it twice,' said Tom. 'The second time was worse.'

'Oh.'

'That was at her flat. There was the most

197

ghastly woman there.'

'Woman?'

'Her flatmate, apparently. How she *could*.'

'Why? What was she like?'

'Ten feet tall, with a cockney accent, and talked entirely in clichés. As far as I could make out, she's a buyer for a department store, and Anne seemed to think it was quite impressive that she frequently goes to Paris.'

'Anne does?'

'No, this – Phyllis. Speaks French with a cockney accent, I suppose.'

'Tom, you sound like a snob!'

'Do I?' He thought it over. 'I suppose I do. It's just that – I thought I knew her. When I went to the rectory at Endersby, it was just what I expected. I could see her there. But that flat – and Phyllis! Anne called her a "bachelor girl," and I can quite see why. It's sort of a spinster's flat, and they live there like a pair of slightly mismatched spinsters. If that's the sort of life she's settled for, it's no wonder we've nothing to say to each other.'

'But did you try to break through?'

'Oh yes, I tried,' said Tom. 'I think she tried, too. But it was no good. Do you remember when Colin was born, we weren't allowed to touch him. He was in a sort of glass dome. We were longing to pick him up

198

and cuddle him, and all we could do was to spread our hands out on the glass and peer at him. It's like that with me and Anne. We peer at each other. But we can't touch each other anymore.'

Pauli coughed discreetly.

'Have you tried to touch her?'

'Oh yes,' said Tom. 'That is...'

'Yes?'

'Do you know what happened on the first evening when I tried to kiss her?'

'She slapped your face?' said Pauli hopefully.

'No,' replied Tom. 'I wish she had. It would at least have shown that she felt *something*. No, she just offered me a chaste cheek.'

'Oh dear,' said Pauli. 'Just good friends, eh?'

'I suppose so,' said Tom. 'But, if so, that's no good to me. That's not how I felt about *her*, and once upon a time it wasn't how *she* felt about *me*.'

Pauli pulled up a couple more weeds and cleaned the trowel with a very earthy forefinger.

'I'd better get the lunch on,' she said. 'David thinks that if he does the shopping on Saturday morning – and does it out of my housekeeping money, I might remark –

199

he has done "a woman's work" for the week.'

She got to her feet.

'Do you want the paper? Oh, I forgot, you read *The Times* now.'

'No,' said Tom. 'I've gone back to the *Daily Telegraph*.'

He thought that Pauli had disappeared inside but heard her voice from the door that led into the kitchen.

'Tom, have you asked her home yet?'

He looked around at her.

'Not likely,' he said. '*I* can't lay on candlelit dinners.'

Pauli stared at him.

'But candlelit dinners is just what you don't want! She's probably shy. Just ask her around to coffee one evening – make it next weekend, when Tiggy and Colin are home for half-term.'

Tom was silent. He felt like a boxer who'd been into the ring twice and got knocked out twice, and felt that was about enough.

'Come on, Tom,' said Pauli lovingly. 'It's worth a try.'

Lucy stared at Tom, aghast.

'Oh, Daddy, *no*!'

'What's the matter?' asked Tom.

'We're going to that birthday party.'

200

'Blast, I'd forgotten.'

Lucy had only just arrived home, and Colin hadn't yet turned up. Pauli had picked Joan and Lucy up from school and taken them back to lunch in Hampshire before dispatching Lucy on to London by train. Colin had travelled from Eastbourne with a school friend and was going to lunch and the cinema with him and his parents. They were getting old enough to have their own engagements now, thought Tom, which meant that he shouldn't take them for granted anymore.

'Never mind,' he said. 'I've invited Miss Hawthorne to drop in for a drink at about six o'clock. At least you'll be able to see her before you leave.'

'Yes,' said Lucy. 'Did you get the pen?'

'The what?'

'Oh, Dad! The birthday present. You said you'd get it.'

'Terribly sorry, Tigs, I forgot.'

'I suppose you were out with Miss Hawthorne,' said Lucy crossly.

'Now, Tigs, it had nothing to do with Miss Hawthorne. I haven't even seen her since ... I've been busy with the sales campaign for the new line, and ever since I got back from Bournemouth, I just haven't stopped.'

'Well,' said Lucy, 'I suppose we can dash

201

out and buy something – that is, if Colin arrives in time. You know what he is!'

A couple of hours later, Anne was standing in the sitting room with a drink in her hand, feeling dazed. She had been slightly puzzled by Tom's invitation to 'drop in for a drink.' Who on earth could pretend to 'drop in for a drink' at Wimbledon on the way from either Southampton Street or South Kensington?'

'Lucy and Colin will be home for term break,' Tom had said, 'and I'd like you to meet them.'

'Lovely,' said Anne.

It really was not a convenient evening at all. She had an urgent editing job that had to be done that weekend to reach the printers by Monday, and she already contemplated working all Saturday and Sunday to complete it in time. It was worth it, though, thought Anne, if she and Tom could meet at last informally and casually, like old friends. And it must mean something if he wanted her to get to know Lucy and Colin, whom she had known so long and so intimately, but never met. She foresaw hopefully, though with some apprehension, a quiet family evening, perhaps with a game of Monopoly or Scrabble.

When the day actually arrived, however,

202

and Anne, with aching feet and a heavy briefcase, having come straight from the office, found herself standing in the Tube after an infuriatingly long wait for a Wimbledon train, her enthusiasm waned. Why should she jump every time Tom telephoned? The war was over, and, damn it, she had her own job, her own – importance. Having studied the map of Wimbledon in the map guide, she began to trudge uphill.

'Tigs,' bellowed Colin from upstairs. 'Have you got the present?'

Lucy's reply was several notes higher, but equally loud.

'It's in your pocket!' she shrieked.

'No, it isn't,' yelled Colin. 'You had it last!'

'No, I didn't! I gave it back to you.'

Tom's voice, from outside the sitting room door, was just as loud as he shouted up to them.

'Shut up, you two!' And then, a fraction more quietly, 'Come down and meet Miss Hawthorne.'

Tom came into the room, glancing backward, and carrying a small dish of peanuts.

'Sorry about this,' he said. 'I'd forgotten that they were going to a birthday party.'

'No, that's quite all right...'

There was thunder of feet on the stairs, and a cheerfully untidy boy explosively entered the room.

'Dad...'

'Come in, Colin,' said Tom unnecessarily. 'This is Miss Hawthorne.'

'How do you do?' said Colin, and in the same breath, 'Tiggy's lost the damn present.'

'Don't swear,' said Tom automatically. 'Obviously one of you has lost the present. It's probably you.'

'You always take her side,' said Colin.

'Not at all.'

Anne caught the resentful flash in Colin's eyes and guessed that he was right. She spoke quickly.

'What present did you get?'

'A pen and pencil set,' answered Colin. 'We dashed out and bought it this evening. He'll probably get forty more, but...'

'If he loses them as quickly as I do...' began Anne, and stopped and laughed. 'Sorry.'

Colin responded to her amusement. He looked just like Tom, with the same humorous grey eyes.

'He's lost this one before he even gets it!' he said.

'Um...' said Anne, in mock hesitation, 'you're sure you've looked in your pockets?'

'Quite sure,' said Colin, feeling in his pockets just the same in a sort of reflex action.

'I suppose,' said Anne, 'you looked in the pockets of the coat you were wearing when you bought it?'

'Oh!' said Colin, and tore out of the room.

Anne turned to smile at Tom and was surprised to see him looking exasperated.

'He's absolutely impossible these days!' he said.

'Oh, Tom! I think he's...'

'Believe it or not, he's on his best behaviour with you,' said Tom. 'Oh, good, here's Lucy. Come in, Tiggy. This is Miss Hawthorne.'

'How do you do?' said Lucy, shaking hands.

'Hello,' said Anne.

Lucy was a surprise. Somehow, Anne had expected a rather sturdy girl with dark, curly hair, like Betty. She remembered the snapshots of Betty that Tom had shown her when they first met, a pleasantly plump, pretty girl with dark hair and, so Tom had told her, hazel eyes. Lucy also had hazel eyes, but her hair was light and fine. In fact, she gave a general impression of being light and fine, a creature of fire and air, like Ariel. Anne was so taken aback that she said the

205

first thing that came into her head.

'I didn't know you were called Tiggy.'

'It's just a family name,' said Tom quickly.

Anne glanced at him, and forced a smile.

'It's all right,' she said. 'I wasn't going to use it.'

She looked back at Lucy.

'My father used to call me "Dumpling,"' she said.

Lucy nodded and smiled but didn't speak. Anne had an uneasy feeling that she was being surveyed and summed up. Colin's voice came from upstairs.

'Got it!' he bellowed.

Anne, Lucy, and Tom looked up and then at each other. Lucy spoke very charmingly and courteously, like the lady of the house.

'I'm terribly sorry, Miss Hawthorne. I'm afraid everything's a bit – a bit hectic.'

'That's quite all right,' replied Anne. 'I gather you're going to a party. I like your dress.'

'Thank you,' said Lucy politely.

Colin's heavy footsteps thundered downstairs, and he came in flourishing a small parcel.

'Found it.'

'So, apologize!' said Lucy.

Colin grinned at Anne, and she grinned back at him.

206

'We'd better go,' he said. 'Are you ready, Tigs?'

'I've been ready for hours,' she said.

'Sure you don't want me to drive you?' asked Tom, putting his arm around Lucy.

She smiled up at him.

'No, Dad, it's only around the corner.' From Tom's arm, she smiled at Anne. 'Good-bye, Miss Hawthorne. Very nice to meet you.'

'Thank you. I hope you have a good party.'

Colin was already out of the room.

'Colin!' shouted Tom. 'Did you say good-bye to Miss Hawthorne?'

Colin put his head around the door and grinned.

'Sorry,' he said. ' 'Bye.'

'Good-bye, Colin,' said Anne, laughing.

Tom followed them out, and Anne heard his voice from the hall.

'Give me a ring if you want me to drive you home.'

'All right, Daddy. ' 'Bye.'

He returned, looking slightly harassed, and went to pour himself a whisky.

'Sorry about Colin,' he said. 'I'm going to have to do something about his manners.'

Anne thought that Lucy's excessively good manners had been much more intimidating but decided not to say so.

'Do sit down,' said Tom.

'I mustn't stay long,' said Anne.

She saw a quick frown of irritation as Tom turned toward her.

'You're always in a rush to get home,' he said. 'What are you going to do tonight? Wash your hair?'

'No,' replied Anne, very precisely, as she sat down on the sofa. 'I have a rather long book to edit. It's due at the printer's on Monday, and if I don't do some work on it tonight, I shall have to sit up until three A.M. tomorrow and Sunday.'

'I do beg your pardon,' said Tom. 'I'd forgotten that you were a big executive.'

Anne felt her temper building up in her and therefore spoke very quietly and calmly.

'I'm not a big executive,' she said. 'I'm simply an editor. But it's my job, and it's important to me.'

'Yes, of course,' said Tom, 'I'm sorry.'

But the tone wasn't exactly apologetic.

'Cheers!' he said, and came and sat down beside her, putting his arm along the back of the sofa.

This is awful, thought Anne as they both drank in silence. I'm sitting next to Tom and we're alone together, and there's nothing to keep us apart. Once upon a time this would have been enough to make us blissfully happy, but all I feel now is embarrassment, and I know he feels the same. What's more, putting his arm along the back of the sofa felt like a rather crude first move in an old-fashioned seduction scene. They might as well be in the back row of the movie theatre.

'You were out when I called on Tuesday evening,' said Tom.

'Was I? Oh yes. So I was.'

'Phyllis said you were "out with Ted."'

'Did she?' said Anne, surprised, and then smiled to herself.

Phyllis, usually discreet to a fault, had evidently decided that Tom could do with a little competition.

'Who's Ted?' asked Tom.

'His name's Edward Brook. He's one of our authors. He's an expert on church architecture. That's really how we – got to know each other.'

'Has he asked you to marry him?' asked Tom.

'Well, really,' said Anne, smiling, 'if he had, I certainly wouldn't tell you!'

Tom suddenly drained his glass and put it down.

'Come on, Anne, I've had enough of this,' he said.

He took her glass from her, and leaned

209

across to put it down on the table beyond her. Then he took hold of her in a masterful manner.

'Darling!' he said, and tried to kiss her.

'No, Tom,' said Anne. 'Tom please – *no*, Tom!'

She struggled free and got to her feet in one furious movement.

'For God's sake!' she exclaimed, 'what's the matter with you?'

Tom stood up, too, confronting her.

'What in hell's the matter with *you*?' he demanded.

'I don't like being mauled about,' said Anne, 'just because you think it's expected of you.'

'Isn't it?' said Tom.

Without a second's hesitation, Anne slapped his face and turned and walked out of the room. She heard Tom's voice behind her.

'Where are you going?'

What a stupid question, thought Anne. She picked up her coat from the chair in the hall and then remembered that she had left her handbag in the sitting room. Tom had followed her to the doorway, and she had to push past him and then scrabble about beside the sofa to find her handbag. It was another stupid anticlimax, like those damn-

210

ed primroses. She found the handbag, picked it up, and turned toward the door.

'Anne...' said Tom.

She waited for him to stand aside and then went out into the hall.

'All right,' said Tom in an exasperated tone of voice, 'if you insist on going, I'll drive you home.'

Anne struggled into her coat, picked up her briefcase, opened the front door and turned to look at him.

'Thank you,' she said, 'I prefer to take the Tube!'

She went out and slammed the door behind her. She was halfway down the path when she heard the door open again and glanced back to see Tom framed in the light.

'Take it, and be damned to you!' he said.

Sixteen

Tom decided to put the whole episode behind him, once and for all. As he sat and waited for Lucy and Colin to come home from their party, he was glad to remember that the school holiday now lasted a week instead of one day as it used to when he went to school. He decided to take a week's holiday himself so that he could spend more time with them. That had been the trouble lately, he thought – he had been neglecting them for his work and for ... this other stupid thing. It had been a wartime romance and, but for the circumstances of their parting, that is how both he and Anne would have thought of it. In fact, if they had gone to bed together and then one or the other of them had been transferred away, he would simply have remembered her as that attractive but rather reserved WAAF officer, with whom he had a brief but charming affair. Now it was over, quite over, and he

212

could acknowledge the fact and take up his normal life again, especially life with his children.

Tom looked at the clock and frowned. The party was being given for a boy who was a year or two older than Lucy. She and Colin had been friends with the whole family ever since they came to Wimbledon, but recently Tom remembered Colin saying Lucy was smitten with Ian, and she had flown at him and furiously denied it, which presumably meant that she *was*. Had she started kissing boys yet? He supposed she had, and he didn't much like the idea. He smiled to himself, wryly. Would he rather she were like Anne, who made such a big thing of it? He thought that, as a father, yes, he would, because it was safer but – wasn't there more to be said for a girl who was warm and generous and maybe ran the risk of being foolish?

All the same, he thought, if Lucy and Colin weren't home in a quarter of an hour, he'd telephone and offer to pick them up in the car, but as he was getting up to fetch his coat, he was relieved to hear the key in the front door.

'Has Miss Hawthorne gone?' asked Colin.

'Good heavens, yes – ages ago,' replied Tom. 'She only dropped in for a drink.'

213

'I liked her,' said Colin. 'She was rather jolly.'

What an extraordinary thing for him to say, thought Tom. If there was one thing that Anne had *not* been that evening, it was 'jolly'!

In the end, Tom didn't take a week's holiday because Lucy and Colin seemed to have made perfectly adequate plans to amuse themselves with their respective friends, and to be quite content otherwise to sleep late in the mornings and play Monopoly in the evenings. But on the last afternoon before they went back, Pauli drove Joan up to London and took her and Lucy shopping. Then they all went out to the Old Vic, where Colin laughed at the funny men but thought there was too much lovey-dovey, and where Lucy and Joan fell deeply in love with the leading actor, John Neville, whom Tom had never heard of.

Next day, when they had seen Colin off on the train to Eastbourne and the girls were upstairs, giggling and packing their suitcases and changing into their school uniform, Tom and Pauli sat and had a cup of coffee.

'Well?' said Pauli. 'What happened?'

'H'm?' said Tom.

'Oh, come on, Tom! That girl – the one

214

you – I don't even know her name.'

'Anne Hawthorne,' said Tom, 'but it don't matter now.'

'Why not? Did you ask her here?'

'Yes,' said Tom grimly, 'I asked her here. The kids were going out to a party, so we sat on the sofa, and I tried to kiss her and got my face slapped.'

'Oh, Tom, you must have done it all wrong!' exclaimed Pauli, with all the just indignation of an elder sister who has given good advice and seen it squandered.

Tom smiled, but he wasn't really amused.

'It's ironic,' he said. 'The first time we parted was the first time I tried to kiss her.'

'And what happened?'

'We tried to keep apart, but we found we loved each other too much.'

'Well, then...'

'It's different this time,' said Tom. 'I was right: she's become a spinster. She has a nice, clean, bare flat and a nice, undemanding, bachelor-girl friend and a nice, simple, educational job – and there's no room in her life for love or sex.'

Pauli, about to drink, put her cup down in the saucer with a clatter.

'How the hell do you know that?' she demanded.

'What?' asked Tom, startled.

215

'How do you know how much sexual desire she has? Just because you grabbed her at the wrong moment...'

'It's not just that,' said Tom. 'I'm pretty sure that she isn't – hasn't...'

'You think she's still a virgin?'

'Yes,' said Tom, 'I do.'

'And you'd rather she'd been whoring about all over the place,' said Pauli, 'hopping in and out of bed with anyone she happened to meet.'

'Yes,' replied Tom defiantly. 'I think I would. At least it would show she was still – still alive.'

Pauli drank her coffee in silence for a moment and then looked up at him.

'But she wouldn't be – Anne Hawthorne, would she?'

'No,' said Tom, 'she wouldn't. So, either way, I've had it.'

There was a shriek of laughter from the girls upstairs, and Pauli got up and went to the door.

'Hurry up, girls!' she called. 'We ought to leave soon.'

She turned back into the room, smiling.

'I wonder if John Neville knows what he's done to them.'

'He's given them an image of romantic love,' said Tom. 'More coffee?'

'Yes. Please.'

She sat down again as Tom, very meticulously, poured each of them another cup of coffee with just the right amount of milk and sugar.

'You know,' he said, 'when we said goodbye in the pub in 1944, and I went outside and got into my car, I kept thinking, "What am I doing, leaving her behind? She's the only girl I'll ever love, and I'm leaving her behind." I kept thinking, "Why don't I just tell the driver to stop and turn around and go back again?" But I didn't. I kept on going, and I left her behind. And that's what I'm doing now.'

He passed Pauli her cup of coffee. She stared at him.

'Then, Tom – for goodness' sake...'

'But now there's a difference. When we said good-bye, she said that we must bury our love so deep that we could never find it again, even if we wanted to. Well, we've done just that. It wasn't only buried. It was dead and buried. We should never had tried to dig it up.'

He heard the girls coming down the stairs, laughing and talking, heavy-footed in their laced-up, flat-heeled shoes, and he looked back to see Pauli's stricken face.

'Oh, Tom,' she said, 'I should never have

meddled. I should have left it alone.'

'I wish to God you had,' he said.

When they had gone, the house was very quiet again. Tom was heating the supper that Lucy had left ready for him when the telephone rang. He stumbled as he ran from his chair into the hall, picked up the telephone, dropped it, juggled with it, and said, 'Hello?'

It was a wrong number.

At about the same time, Anne was returning to her flat with Edward Brook. They had been to a perfectly appalling literary party – that is, it had been even more appalling than most literary parties, and Ted had proved to be the perfect escort. He had kept her glass filled without once disappearing for twenty minutes, while she stood alone in the middle of the room wondering if she would ever see him again. He was an excellent forager, always discovering the smoked salmon and the piping-hot liver and bacon rolls. Never did he produce, with an air of triumph, a plate of cold, pallid sausage rolls, in which the pastry contrived to be at once heavy and crumbling, and the small, pale sausage gave an unhappy feeling of eating someone's little finger.

Even better, since one had one's grim duty

to do at these parties, he didn't pen her, guiltily if enjoyably, in a corner, but shared with her the rare and joyful gift of hunting in pairs. This consisted of identifying celebrities and bores, giving each his due mead of attention and flattery and then, by unspoken consent, drifting quietly on. This last gift was even more valuable when, as so often happened, the celebrity was a bore. They even managed to talk for a considerable time to the author, without ever giving him cause to guess that they thought his book, which they were there to celebrate, was the most pretentious and tedious ever written.

'We have now,' said Anne, in the voice of Lady Catherine de Bourgh, 'done our duty in every conceivable way and, in my opinion, should now depart with all convenient speed.'

'Shall we go and have dinner?' asked Ted as they headed unobtrusively for the exit.

'I couldn't. That last liver and bacon roll was positively the one over the limit. Come back to the flat and have a cup of coffee.'

Phyllis had just left for a week in Paris to steal next winter's fashions, and that was a relief. Her heroic avoidance of the subject of Tom was beginning to get on Anne's nerves.

'I must find another flat,' she thought, as

219

Ted waited for her to open the front door.

Anne was glad that he didn't try to take the key and do it for her. No doubt it was a charmingly old-fashioned romantic custom, like arriving with a bunch of flowers, but it made her feel she was considered too much of an idiot to be capable of opening the door herself.

'I hope you don't mind Nescafé,' said Anne.

'I much prefer it,' he replied. 'I wish all my friends would use it instead of making bad coffee and boasting about it.'

Anne laughed. They had both had just enough to drink to make them cheerful without being silly. He came into the kitchen with her, and they talked about the party and the people there, and then he carried the tray into the sitting room, and they sat and drank coffee very companionably. When Ted put his cup down and turned to her and spoke with a change of tone, he took her by surprise.

'Anne,' he said, 'you and I get on awfully well together.'

'Yes,' replied Anne, smiling, 'I suppose we do.'

He reached for her.

'Oh, Ted!' said Anne, irritated, as she spilled coffee on her new dress.

'Anne, darling...'

'Ted!' cried Anne, putting down her cup and wiping her dress, 'please don't be a bore.'

'You must have known I was falling in love with you,' he said.

Anne looked at him, startled.

'No,' she answered guiltily, 'I don't think I did.'

She got up and went to the kitchen to sponge off her dress. It wasn't very romantic, but it was a new dress, and if she didn't wipe the coffee off at once, it would stain. Ted followed her to the doorway. She looked up and saw him.

'Can't we just – go on as we are?' she said.

'You mean – just good friends?'

'Yes,' replied Anne warmly.

She dried the dress with a clean dish towel and came toward him. Ted put his hand on her shoulder and looked down at her gravely.

'No,' he said. 'I don't think we can.'

She walked on past him into the sitting room, but he followed and took her in his arms.

'No, Ted...'

'You know the trouble with you?'

'No,' said Anne, teasing him, 'what's the trouble with me?'

'You're afraid of love,' said Ted.

He bent to kiss her.

'No, Ted,' said Anne. 'Please don't.'

She freed herself and walked away. When he spoke, the tone of his voice had altered.

'Is there someone else?' he asked.

She turned, looked at him, and hesitated.

'There – was.'

'Was,' he repeated. 'Then there's hope for me.'

She hesitated again.

'No,' she answered sadly. 'No, I'm sorry, Ted, not really.'

They stood and looked at each other for a long time in silence.

When Ted had gone, Anne meticulously washed up the coffee cups and put them away. She stood and looked around the bare, clean flat, and thought it resembled a WAAF officer's quarters – or a women's prison.

'I must get a flat of my own,' she thought.

She rather fancied Chelsea. It would be quite fun to furnish it according to her own taste and really settle into it, make it her home. She wouldn't tell Tom that she was moving. He could always look her up later in the telephone directory if he wanted to, but she knew he wouldn't. If he rang the flat once and found she had gone away, that

222

would be the end of it. She turned toward her bedroom but, in response to one of those obscure subliminal electronic messages from the brain, she paused and picked up her handbag. Sitting down, she opened it and took out her wallet. Still responding to that sleepwalking compulsion, she felt behind her driver's license and her old identity card and drew out a snapshot. It showed Tom, in uniform, outside The Reed Thatcher. He looked very young, and he was smiling. So vivid was her memory of that moment that she actually remembered looking at him in the viewfinder of her box camera.

'Say "cheese,"' she had said, as he later said to her, and then he laughed, and she took the picture.

She sat and looked at it for a long time, and she didn't really feel anything except the memory of a calm and distant sorrow. At last she put the photograph away and went to bed.

Seventeen

The doorbell rang so loudly that Anne thought it was a fire alarm. It must have struck a subconscious conditioned response because she imagined that she was back on the station. She was out of bed and in the middle of the room, thinking that she must get her WAAFs safely outside, before she came to and wondered where she was. The doorbell had stopped, and she stood still, trying to get her wits together. Then it began again.

Clutching her dressing gown around her, Anne cautiously opened the door and saw Tom.

'Come on,' he said, 'we're going for a drive.'

'What? Do you know what time it is?'

'No idea,' said Tom. 'I've been up all night.'

He came inside.

'Hurry up and get dressed,' he said.

Anne stared at him.

'You must be mad.'

'I am,' said Tom. 'As mad as hell. Come on, Anne, I've had enough of this rubbish.'

Anne closed the door. She still felt dazed.

'Do you want a cup of tea?' she asked.

'No, we'll have it at a café, as soon as we get out of London. Buck up and get dressed.'

He spoke to her in the tone of a senior officer addressing a junior one, and partly because she was still not quite awake and therefore operating on instinct, she obeyed.

There wasn't time to think about dressing smartly. She took the first clothes that came to hand – a plain suit and sweater and a belted raincoat. When she came out, Tom was standing exactly where she'd left him.

'That was quick,' he said and grinned.

Almost against her will she smiled back at him, and he put an arm around her shoulders.

'Come on,' he said.

They hardly spoke again until they were on the Kingston bypass, and then Tom said without turning his head, 'Why do you always keep that flat so tidy?'

'It's awful, isn't it?' said Anne.

He threw a quick glance at her, and she saw the relief in his face.

'It belongs to Phyllis, really,' said Anne.

225

'She advertised for a flatmate, and I wanted somewhere to live. She liked it to look like a hospital waiting room.'

'I noticed,' said Tom. 'How on earth do you put up with it?'

'I don't really care,' said Anne. 'I've never thought of it as home. It was just somewhere to camp out until...'

'Until...?'

'Until nothing,' said Anne.

Tom turned the car off the road.

'There's a good roadside café here,' he said. 'I used to come here when I was a travelling salesman.'

'I didn't know you'd ever been a travelling salesman,' said Anne, surprised.

Tom stopped the car in the rough yard.

'You never asked,' he said.

The café was full of truck drivers, those most discriminating of connoisseurs, all having breakfast.

'Mm,' said Anne. 'Hot buttered toast!'

'Sure you wouldn't like a bacon sandwich?'

'I'd like both!' said Anne.

Tom escorted her to the only empty table. She thought that the truck drivers looked at them with some resentment until Tom approached the counter and the woman who was pouring tea exclaimed, 'Tom! 'Ow

226

are yer? 'Aven't seen you for ages!'

'All right, Kath,' answered Tom. 'I'm not on the road anymore.'

'Oh, moved up in the world, 'ave yer? I suppose you'll want champagne now.'

'Two nice cups of tea will do,' answered Tom, 'that is, if you're making a fresh pot.'

'You'll take what you get and like it!' said Kath, and Anne laughed and caught the eye of one of the truck drivers at the next table, and saw him grinning too.

When Tom returned to the table while Kath made the toast and bacon sandwiches, Anne said, 'You said you'd seen Bender. How was he?'

'Not eating bacon sandwiches,' said Tom, and Anne realized that for the first time since they had met again, their minds were running along the same path.

'He was rather sad, really, I suppose,' Tom added, 'except that...'

'What?'

The mirth that had been halved because it wasn't shared suddenly overtook Tom.

'They live in a house in the suburbs of Birmingham which looks as if it belongs in the Ideal Home Exhibition, and Bender was terribly embarrassed because he always cooks their high tea...'

'High tea?'

'Quite customary up north,' said Tom solemnly. 'And that night it was kippers, but he'd only got two.'

'*Kippers?*'

'Mavis did apologize for the smell.'

They were both, shamefully, convulsed with laughter.

The toast and sandwiches were superb, and Kath *had* made a fresh pot of tea. While Tom was paying the three and nine (Kath had thrown in two extra cups of tea for nothing, for old time's sake) Anne caught the eye of the truck driver, who gave a great wink. And, as she reached the door, Kath said, 'Bye, bye, dear. All the best.'

'Thank you,' said Anne.

She remembered the RAF warrant officer who, after she had covered up an appalling but inadvertent breach of discipline by one of his aircraftsmen, had invited her into the sergeants' mess for a drink. To be accepted into some societies meant a great deal more than being allowed into the royal enclosure at Ascot, and this was one of them. Kath's words, 'All the best,' followed her out to the car as a kind of benediction.

Anne fell asleep after breakfast and only woke up when Tom turned onto a country road winding uphill and brought the car to a halt in the entrance to a field looking out over the downs.

'Why are we stopping?' asked Anne, un-surprised at anything by this time. 'Have you brought a picnic?'

'No,' answered Tom, 'but the pubs aren't open yet.'

If she had not been sure before, Anne knew now for certain where they were going. Tom took her hand in his and settled back and closed his eyes.

'They've got a new sign,' said Anne as they drove into the concrete parking lot.

The old Reed Thatcher, who had looked so mellow and friendly, had been replaced by a shiny, brightly coloured, phony country bumpkin with lustrous red cheeks, who looked down on them with a leer. They got out of the car and headed for the door. Tom paused and looked back.

'There used to be a gun emplacement over there,' he said.

'It looked better than the parking lot,' said Anne. 'More civilized.'

'Much,' Tom agreed, and pushed the door open for her.

The pub was empty, and the piece of aircraft fuselage that used to hang over the bar had given way to horse-brasses, pro-bably made in Birmingham. The oak beams had been varnished, and someone had put an oriental carpet down on the floor. There was even a jukebox.

'If you ask me,' said Tom under his breath, 'this pub has changed hands.'

A sour-looking landlord emerged from the door at the back of the bar. He seemed surprised to see them and not too pleased, as though he had not expected customers.

'Morning,' he said.

'Good morning,' said Tom. 'A gin and lime and a whisky and soda, please.'

The landlord nodded and turned to get two glasses, then paused.

'Gin and lime? You sure you don't mean gin and tonic?'

'Definitely gin and lime,' answered Tom, taking Anne's elbow and steering her to a table in the window.

'It's very quiet,' she said, as they sat and waited for the drinks.

'No Lancs going home,' said Tom.

A blackbird was singing outside the window, and Anne glanced toward it.

'I suppose the birds were always singing,' she said, 'but we couldn't hear them.'

'At least we can hear them now,' said Tom. She glanced up and smiled at him. The landlord came over with the drinks.

'Where's Frank?' inquired Tom.

'Who?'

'Frank Baker.'

'Never heard of him.'

'He used to be landlord. How long've you been here?'

'Six years!' said the landlord indignantly.

'Time flies,' said Tom, glancing at Anne.

'You cannot,' replied Anne instantly. 'They fly too quickly.'

Tom's mouth fell open.

'That's a *terrible* joke!' he said.

'Do you think so?' said Anne, wounded. 'It used to be a favourite of mine.'

'There's a lot I don't know about you,' said Tom, shaking his head.

The landlord turned away with a final dubious look at them over his shoulder. Tom took hold of his drink with his right hand, and Anne took hold of hers with her left. Their other hands met beneath the table and clasped tightly.

'I've been trying to find you for a long time,' said Tom. 'I even put an ad in the personal column of *The Times*.'

'I read the *Telegraph*.'

'And I never thought of that,' said Tom. 'I was sure you'd read *The Times*.'

'Daddy used to read it.'

'I was looking for you, not Daddy!' said Tom and then, 'Oh, darling I'm so sorry!'

It was the first time he had called her

231

'darling' in the old way, and he wasn't embarrassed about her father's death, just openly annoyed with himself for his clumsiness, so that Anne responded with unfeigned ease and simplicity.

'That's all right.' She added, after a pause, 'Tom, I've never said properly how sorry I was about Betty. It must have been an awful shock for you – and for the children.'

'Yes, it was. I never knew what a shock death was before. People died in the war, but it wasn't the same somehow.'

'No,' Anne agreed. 'It wasn't just that there wasn't time to think about it. It was more that when the war began, you sort of – gave everyone up for dead, including yourself. Afterward, you counted up how many of your friends you'd lost, but then it was too late for shock – almost too late for sorrow.'

'Still,' said Tom, 'your father's death must have been a shock for you.'

'Only because it was sudden.'

She was blessedly glad to talk about her father's death. There'd been no one to confide in at the time, and now to be able to talk about it to Tom...

'He really wanted to go,' she said. 'He was tired out. No one realizes what a hard life a country parson has – up early, snatched meals, trudging about the parish in all weather like a ploughman. And that's quite apart from the fearsome spiritual struggle of trying to convey the Faith to your people when you're only hanging on to your own by the skin of your teeth.'

'I never thought of that,' said Tom.

'And at last,' said Anne, 'he homeward wended his weary way.'

She freed her hand to get her handkerchief out to wipe her eyes, and Tom put a comforting arm around her shoulder.

'Do you know,' she said, 'the night he died, he was trying to write his sermon for next day. He'd been struggling with it for hours. I know, because he started directly after supper and I said good night to him about eleven, and when I found him next morning, he'd only got as far as the text: 'God is faithful!'

'You put that on his tombstone!' Tom exclaimed.

She looked at him, startled.

'How do you know?'

'I went to Norfolk looking for you.'

'You did?' cried Anne, delighted.

'I met Mrs Wilton.'

'Oh, Tom, did you really?'

'And there was a very sharp forward-looking young rector. He and Mrs Wilton hated

233

each other.'

'Oh, I *am* glad,' cried Anne, unregenerate. 'But, if you were looking for me, I left an address with Mrs Ainsworth...'

'Fanny Ainsworth. Yes, I know. But where had Fanny Ainsworth gone? Bloody Australia, that's where?'

'Oh, Tom!' cried Anne, suddenly convulsed with laughter, 'I wish I'd been there!'

'Well, if you had been, I wouldn't have been traipsing all over the country looking for you, would I?' said Tom, outraged.

'True,' replied Anne apologetically.

Tom tossed off his drink, and because he didn't want to take his arm away from Anne, he called out, 'Landlord!' The landlord, polishing glasses, looked at him resentfully, and the two or three local customers who were standing at the bar turned with that slow, hostile stare that is the mark of the really bad, unfriendly pub.

'I wonder what his name is,' murmured Anne, as the landlord raised the ledge of the bar.

''Orrible 'Erbert,' said Tom, just as the man arrived beside them. 'Er – same again?'

'No,' said Anne, overcoming a giggle, 'gin and lime really *is* awfully sweet and sticky. I think I'd like a gin and tonic.'

'And a half of bitter,' said Tom to 'Orrible

'Erbert. 'And could we have some sandwiches?'

'We don't do sandwiches,' said the landlord.

They looked at him solemnly.

'Just as a special favour?' said Anne, 'because we're such *very* old customers?'

He scowled.

'You can have some bread and cheese,' he said.

'You spoil us,' remarked Anne soulfully, and she felt Tom's hand grip hers under the table.

'I forgot to tell you,' said Tom. 'I met someone else in Endersby. His name was Alf, and he was a great admirer of yours. He was the one who told me you'd gone to Cambridge – though he thought it might be Oxford.'

'Dear Alf,' said Anne, 'how was he? And it was Newnham College, Cambridge.'

'So I found out.'

'Don't tell me you went to Cambridge, too!'

'No, I wrote to them. But they only knew your old address.'

'Newnham never really became part of my life,' said Anne thoughtfully, 'except for the Family.'

She told him about the Newnham Family

235

and was delighted that he understood and that she could share them with him.

The landlord brought the drinks, and a woman who looked even more disagreeable than he did emerged from the door behind the bar and produced a plate of bread, butter, and cheese. 'Orrible 'Erbert brought it over to them, and Tom, to Anne's undisguised admiration, bravely asked for pickles as well.

'Anything else?' asked the landlord.

'No thanks,' answered Tom. 'We're all right now,' and added as the man moved away, 'to coin a phrase.'

'Oh,' cried Anne. 'I thought you'd forgotten that; Guiseppi asked if we were all right, and you said yes, and we weren't at all. Wasn't that an awful evening?'

'Quite appalling,' said Tom. 'And you'd done your hair in a funny way.'

'Not at all. It just had a – a golden rinse.'

'Ah. I thought it was dyed.'

'How dare you!' exclaimed Anne in the middle of a bite of crusty bread, spilling crumbs down the front of her sweater. 'It was supposed to make me more attractive to you. *And* I had on my best dress.'

'I noticed,' said Tom. 'It was very revealing.'

Anne saw his eyes looking at her bosom as

236

she dusted the crumbs off it.

'And did you object to that too?' she inquired.

'Yes, I think I did,' said Tom reflectively. 'I can't imagine why.'

'Let's go back to that restaurant,' said Anne. 'Let's allow the waiter to fuss over us as much as he likes, and I'll flirt with him, and you...'

'I hope you don't expect me to flirt with Guiseppi!' said Tom.

They both laughed, and Anne realized suddenly that all the disasters of their reunion had now become part of their shared amusement – even part of their love. Perhaps that was what she had forgotten, that love was shared jokes as well as shared joys and sorrows.

'Oh, Tom!' she said.

'What?'

'Nothing. Just, oh, Tom.'

When they had finished their bread and cheese, they sat and held hands and they knew, without needing to say so, that they were both seeing the old wartime pub and the young fighter pilots who laughed so much and were afraid and many of whom never came home again.

'I suppose,' said Tom unexpectedly, 'that you would like the Benders to come to our wedding?'

Anne looked at him, startled.

'Is that a proposal of marriage?'

'Not likely!' said Tom. 'When *I* make a proposal of marriage, you'll know it, but that won't be until I know how you feel about it. I might get my face slapped.'

'If that's what you want, Tom Sanders,' said Anne, threateningly, 'you're going the right way about it!'

They became aware of the landlord raising the ledge of the counter and approaching them.

'I've got to close now,' he said.

'What?'

His wife was peering at them from behind the bar, and everyone else had gone.

'It's closing time,' said 'Orrible 'Erbert.

'Oh,' said Tom.

The landlord took their glasses and plates and went to put them on the bar, glancing back at them.

'Well, I suppose...' said Tom.

'Yes,' said Anne.

They disengaged their hands still looking at each other.

'That doodlebug nearly got us after all,' said Tom.

'Very nearly,' said Anne.

The landlord followed them to the door

and closed it behind them, and they turned to each other in that embrace that had formerly been denied them.

'Hello, darling,' he said.

'Hello.'

They heard the bolt shot home on the door of The Reed Thatcher, but they didn't care. They would probably never go there again.

'Darling Anne,' said Tom, 'you will marry me, won't you?'

'Oh, Tom, I want to so much, but...'

'But...?'

'Colin and Lucy – do you think they'll mind?'

'If *that's* all you're worrying about...' exclaimed Tom, laughing, 'it was Lucy who helped me to find you again.'

Eighteen

Because the school term was a short one, they agreed to wait and tell Colin and Lucy the news when they came home for the Easter holidays. Meanwhile, for the very first time since they met, they were able to spend time together without any shadow of guilt or subterfuge. It was a time of such happiness that Anne – puritan to the last – thought that it could not really be allowed, that something must happen, sooner or later, to spoil it.

Oddly enough, one contributing factor to their enjoyment was the fact that they were both so busy with their respective jobs that their time together was still stolen time. They even made those absurd snatched and secret lovers' telephone calls from the office. Often it was just, 'Anne?' 'Tom.' 'I love you.' Sometimes it was a teasing, 'Tom Sanders here.' 'Who?'

They took turns buying and cooking supper. They would have it at Anne's flat if

Phyllis was out, because it was nearer to where they both worked. They laughed ruefully over the fact that while Tom was desperately searching for her they were actually spending most of their working days within a few streets of each other.

'I usually took the bus home,' said Anne.

'I took the Tube.'

And they thought of all the Londoners in the rush hour, conditioned, like ants to stream down the steps into the Underground, or to stand, evening paper in hand, at the bus stop, and thought that they might even have brushed past each other and never met, and trembled at the thought.

If Phyllis was in the flat, then they had their supper at Wimbledon, and Anne, knowing that this would be their home after they were married, felt a subtle pleasure in taking tentative possession of it. Now and then when Tom was home late, she would wander silently about the house that was not yet hers, but Betty's. It seemed important that she should get to know the house while it still belonged to Betty, in order to justify her inheritance and prepare for the moment when the house became hers – if that moment ever came. Then she would hear Tom's key in the latch, and she would run to welcome him home. Once he was there the make-believe vanished, and the house belonged to both of them. And if they were eating at Wimbledon, he would never let her travel home alone but drove her by car or sometimes came with her in the Tube to South Kensington. And because they travelled in it together, hand in hand, that swaying, dirty, ill-lit Underground train, with its wartime air of griminess and squalor, acquired a spurious air of romance, like a scene from a French film.

And, whether at the flat or Wimbledon, when they had finished supper, they would wash up, pleasurably together, talking all the time about the day's doings.

'That pathetic little man came in today.'

'The one who wanted you to publish his autobiography?'

'Yes, wasn't it awful? I was going to return it to him with a nice letter, but as it was, I had to put that great bundle into his arms and try to explain that we couldn't publish it, and the brown paper wrapping came off, and half the untidy mass of ill-written rubbish fell on the floor. There we both were, trying to pick it up, with me still trying to explain and him still saying, "Why?" I couldn't say, "Because it's vilely written, and you've had a deadly dull life, and no one would be interested." But in the end I almost had to say just that because he wouldn't take no far an answer.'

'Like Perkins.'

'Oh dear! Your Birmingham salesman. Don't say, he's still...'

'He actually came to the office today.'

'Oh, *no!*'

The amazing thing was that now that they were actually talking about it, they found that their jobs had much in common. Books had to be sold, just as much as office furniture, and a dud article or a good article that the public didn't want or that was priced out of its market was the same in both lines of work. And since they both enjoyed what they were doing, they each found enormous double pleasure – quadrupled pleasure – in talking about their own business and sharing each other's.

'I'd like to go on working after we're married,' said Anne, 'although...'

She stopped.

'You're blushing,' said Tom.

'I'm not!' cried Anne indignantly.

They were sharing the big armchair, with *The Black and White Minstrel Show* turned low on television.

'Out with it,' said Tom.

'Well – I would like to have a baby.'

She glanced up and caught the look on

243

his face.

'Oh dear,' she said, 'you'd hate it.'

'Well...' he said dubiously.

'I know. Starting another family, and putting up with nappies and broken nights and ...Would you really hate it?'

'I don't know,' answered Tom. 'Because of the war, I never really knew the children until they were on their feet and walking. But I do know one thing.'

He looked fondly down at her.

'What's that?'

'I know that, loving each other as we do, we ought to have our own baby.'

'Oh, I'm so glad you feel like that!' cried Anne. 'The Family used to say...'

'The Newnham Family.'

'Yes,' said Anne, smiling. 'The men at Cambridge were mostly such a dead loss. They were either callow youths straight from school, who were *years* younger than we were, or else they were ex-officers, rather pompous and only intent on getting their degrees and bustling off into politics. Their way of preparing for *that* was to talk uninterrupted and never listen to anyone.'

'So you didn't have any romantic episodes at Cambridge?' inquired Tom.

'Well – one,' answered Anne. 'But it was no good, you see, because I was still in love with you.'

'I can see I've got a lot to answer for,' said Tom, and was only half joking. He kissed her and added, 'You never told me what the Family said.'

'Oh – well, we all agreed that we didn't really want to get married...'

'Really?'

'Not *then*, but we did want children. So we said, the thing to do was to find some convenient and not altogether repulsive man, spend the night with him, and then say, "Thank you very much, good night, and goodbye," and trot away with a nice baby of our own.'

'But you never quite got around to it?' asked Tom.

'We-ell,' replied Anne, remembering Charles Prendergast and smiling reminiscently, 'not *quite*.'

'Look here, young Anne,' said Tom, 'you'd better take that look off your face until our wedding night. That is,' he added, 'if we're really going to wait until...'

'Yes, we *are*,' said Anne and struggled free, breathless and laughing. 'I haven't waited all this time to lose my virtue now, almost within sight of the altar!'

Colin was arriving home the day before Lucy, and since Tom had to go to the new factory at High Wycombe, Anne offered to meet him. She felt extremely nervous, but in fact Colin seemed delighted to see her, ate a large meal of fish and chips in the Chicken Inn, and enjoyed a visit to the zoo as much as she did. In the evening Tom cooked sausages and baked beans, which Colin, a lad of simple tastes, assured Anne was his favourite meal after fish and chips. Then they all played Monopoly and Colin won handsomely.

'I must go,' said Anne. 'I'm broke, anyway.'

Tom followed her out into the hall and helped her into her coat.

'I'll drive you,' he said, glancing back at Colin still happily counting his Monopoly money. 'He'll be all right for an hour.'

'Certainly not,' said Anne, looking up at him over her shoulder. 'We have a family now.'

He drew her around into his arms and, out of sight of Colin, they had their last secret kiss.

Pauli drove the girls up to London the next day. David had come up by train for an appointment at the War Office, and Pauli and Joan were going to pick him up later and drive back to Hampshire. Anne had agreed to join them for lunch.

'It'll give you a chance to meet Pauli,' said Tom, 'and then you can stay on afterward and we'll tell the children.'

'Don't you think Lucy would rather have her first evening alone with you?' said Anne.

'Chicken!' accused Tom, and because there was some truth in it, and she *was* dreading breaking the news of their marriage to Colin and Lucy, Anne agreed.

Meeting Pauli was quite a sufficient ordeal. She and the girls had just arrived when Anne walked up from the station, and Lucy was in the hall with Tom.

'Tigs, you remember Miss Hawthorne,' said Tom with a note of pride.

'Oh – yes,' replied Lucy. 'Yes, of course.'

She spoke pleasantly enough, but with a slightly puzzled look that plainly inquired what on earth Anne was doing there. Tom should have written to her, thought Anne miserably, or at least told her quietly on his own. We're doing this all wrong.

Pauli was large but trim, wearing good country tweeds and a slightly military beret on her neat greying hair. Anne remembered Tom telling her that Pauli had been extremely bright as a girl and went to college-preparatory school and then into the civil service before meeting David. She had the air of someone who had always managed

247

her own life very well and did her best to manage everyone else's. Anne knew that Tom had told her that they were engaged but had asked her to keep quiet about it until the children knew.

'Glad to meet you,' Pauli said. 'Tom's told me so much about you.'

There was an appraising look as she shook hands, and Anne decided to challenge it.

'And am I what you expected?' she asked.

There was a little flash of surprise in Pauli's eyes before she answered.

'I'm not sure,' she said thoughtfully.

They both laughed, and Anne thought, we're going to be friends. How marvelous!

Lunch at the local restaurant was a cheerful affair. The girls were in the high spirits which came from being released from boarding school, but they still had not quite left it behind. They kept relapsing into the deliciously silly schoolgirl chatter, like travellers from abroad who keep breaking into a foreign language, but this was a language no adult could understand. Over the ice cream they argued passionately about the merits of a singer called Frankie Lane.

'Frankie Lane's a pill,' said Colin, rashly entering the fray.

'Colin thinks everyone's a pill,' said Lucy.

'No, I don't,' answered Colin. 'I don't think Anne's a pill.'

'Oh, thank you!' said Anne, laughing. 'I *am* honored.'

She glanced at Tom and saw his look of pride and pleasure, then, as she quickly looked away, caught sight of Lucy's watchful gaze.

When they got back to the house, all was confusion. Pauli was trying to disentangle Lucy's possessions from the trunk of the car and to detach Joan from a conversation with her cousin, which, one might have thought, could have taken place at any time during the past two months but which had suddenly become urgent.

'Come on, darling,' begged Pauli. 'Daddy will be standing outside the War Office, jumping up and down.' And, seeing Joan slowly detaching herself, she said quietly to Anne, 'I'm *so* glad. Good luck – especially with Lucy.'

Then Pauli and Joan were gone, and Anne was standing somewhat dazed, inside the house while Colin and Lucy wrangled noisily, as they had done on her first evening there.

'I'm going to phone Smudge.'

'You can't! I need the phone.'

'Going to call Ian, I suppose!'

'No, I'm not, you little squirt. I promised to call Sally as soon as I got back. Don't bother! I might as well go over there.'

'I might as well go to Smudge's house. 'Bye, Anne.'

'Oh, yes. Good-bye, Miss Hawthorne. See you later, Dad.'

Suddenly they had both abandoned the telephone and were heading for the front door.

'Wait a minute!' called Tom.

They paused, looking back.

'We've something to tell you,' said Tom, and took Anne's hand and turned aside into the sitting room.

When Lucy and Colin arrived, dubiously, in the doorway, Tom and Anne were standing hand in hand in the middle of the room.

'Anne and I are getting married,' said Tom.

Colin's response was unexpected.

'I knew it!' he shouted, turning triumphantly to Lucy.

'How?' she demanded. 'How did you know it?'

'I just did, that's all.'

He looked at Anne.

'Are you a good cook?'

'Well,' said Anne, 'I'm not bad, as long as I keep clear of mushrooms.'

She looked at Tom, and they both smiled. Anne looked back at Colin and Lucy and saw them both now solemn-faced.

'I hope you don't mind,' she said.

'What shall we call you?' inquired Colin. 'Stepmother?'

'Ugh, no, I don't think so. And you're too grown-up to call me "Aunt Anne." Why don't you just stick to "Anne"?'

'Are you sure you wouldn't prefer "Dumpling"?' asked Lucy.

Anne thought at first it was a joke, but then glanced at Lucy and saw that it wasn't. She forced a smile.

'No, I don't think I fancy that too much,' she said, 'that is, unless I can call you "Tigs."'

'Not bloody likely!' said Lucy.

'Tigs!' said Tom, shocked.

Lucy didn't look at him. She kept her eyes fixed on Anne.

'I think it's absolutely disgusting!' she said. 'You were carrying on together all through the war...'

'Tigs!'

She still looked only at Anne.

'Even when Mummy was dying, Daddy was thinking about *you*.'

'Tigs, please!' said Tom. 'That's not true.'

He moved to put his arm around her, but

251

Lucy evaded him and was out in the hall, glaring at them.

'I think it's disgusting!' she said and burst into tears and ran upstairs. Her bedroom door slammed.

Anne thought that Tom would telephone as soon as she arrived home. She half expected it to be ringing as she walked in the door. But the hours went by, and still it had not rung.

'Oh, deary me!' said Phyllis, coming in at eleven o'clock. 'I'm going to have to give up going out with Gareth. These concerts are killing me. You don't tell me anyone really *enjoys* them. D'you want a cup of tea?'

'Mm, love one,' said Anne – and then the telephone rang.

'Anne?' said Tom.

Anne looked at Phyllis.

'Don't mind me,' said Phyllis. 'I'll put the kettle on.' She went into the kitchen and shut the door.

'Anne?'

Tom's voice was lowered, as though he was afraid of being overheard.

'Hello, Tom.'

'Sorry I haven't called before,' he said.

'Yes, I was waiting.'

'I know. Sorry. I couldn't ring until Lucy

252

was in bed and asleep.'

'Oh.'

'Lucy' she noticed. Not 'Tiggy.'

'We must talk,' said Tom.

'Yes,' said Anne, 'I think we should.'

'The thing is, darling...'

'Tom,' Anne interrupted. 'Are you calling from the hall?'

'No, from the study.'

'Then, for God's sake, stop whispering!'

'I'm not whispering!' said Tom loudly and angrily.

'Fine,' said Anne. 'Go on.'

'I've got that sales conference all tomorrow and then the dinner in the evening. The day after...'

'The day after is Good Friday,' said Anne. 'I'll be going to church.'

'Oh, yes. Well – I'll come and see you in the evening.'

'Wouldn't it be better,' said Anne, 'for us all to meet together and talk it over?'

'No,' said Tom. 'No, I don't think so. Tiggy's really upset. Let's give her a chance to calm down. All right?'

Anne was silent for a long time.

'All right,' she said and put the phone down.

They hadn't even said, 'I love you.'

Anne sat looking at the telephone, and the

253

familiar feelings of defeat and despair crept over her. Betty had won after all. And then ... Really! she thought. What a stupid and melodramatic thing to say! Betty was dead. She had been the innocent victor in a battle she never knew she was fighting, but now she was dead and, as in that other, greater war, she and Tom had already taken possession of the liberated continent. They were not going to be defeated now by a charming but spoiled little pocket of resistance called Lucy.

Perhaps it would have been different if this had happened before she and Tom went back to The Reed Thatcher, before they spent the ensuing weeks together in such joy and closeness. Now she knew they had something to lose. Tom couldn't put up much of a struggle, hampered by the slightly guilty thought of his dead wife and by his love for his daughter.

'But *I* damn well can!' thought Anne.

She remembered saying to Tom, 'Please don't swear,' and laughed aloud. Perhaps it's about time I did start swearing, she thought.

Phyllis put her heard around the door and saw that she was off the telephone.

'Would you like your cup now, dear?'

'Yes, please,' said Anne.

She got up and walked to the doorway of

the kitchen.

'Phyllis,' she said, 'did you ever meet the man you thought was worth fighting for?'

'Not me, dear.'

Phyllis paused, teapot in hand.

'You know something? I don't think I'm really the marrying kind.'

'Well, I *am*!' said Anne.

Anne didn't sit down in the train on the way to Wimbledon the next evening. She stood, holding the upright bar and staring straight ahead. She had that peculiar wartime feeling that this was not her but someone else taking these awful chances, and that one day she would look back and say, 'Did I do that? How could I? How did I live through it?' Walking up the hill was hard, but the worst part was standing outside the door of the house and forcing herself to ring the bell. Lucy opened the door on the chain.

'Oh,' she said. 'My father's out.'

'Yes, I know,' said Anne. 'I wanted to see *you*. May I come in?'

Lucy closed the door, and for a moment Anne thought that she was actually going to shut her out. Then she realized that Lucy had to close the door to take the chain off. But as she stepped inside, she knew that the chain might be down but that all Lucy's mental and emotional chains were in place.

255

'I'd like to talk to you alone,' she said.

Lucy shrugged.

'Colin's out,' she said, and led the way into the sitting room.

They stood and looked at each other. Anne had planned what she was going to say, so it wasn't too difficult to begin.

'You said we were "carrying on" during the war,' said Anne, 'but that's exactly what we didn't do. We fell in love – we couldn't help that – but because your father was married, we parted. That didn't just happen. We made the decision and it was agonizing. We didn't go to bed together. We parted, lived separate lives, never saw each other. Now we've met again, and we find that we're still in love – or maybe we've fallen in love again. Anyway, we're not going to be parted again, not by you, not by anyone.'

Lucy stood and looked back at her in stony silence.

'Oh, please, Lucy,' cried Anne. 'You're going to fall in love yourself quite soon and get married. And even before that you'll go to university or get a job, probably move into a flat of your own. Don't you think it would be selfish to use your father's love for you to insist that he should stay here alone?'

'You're not thinking about that,' said Lucy sharply. 'It's not him you're thinking about.

You want him for yourself.'

Anne couldn't deny it. It was true.

'All right,' she said. 'I do. And what's more, I'm older now and a lot tougher. If I have to, I'll fight you for him. But I don't want to – and I know your mother wouldn't want it, either.'

Lucy flared up at that.

'You've no right to talk about her!' she said.

'I've every right,' answered Anne. 'I never met her, but she's part of my life just as you are. Your father talked about her from the day we met. He loved her...'

'Not as much as she loved him,' Lucy broke in. 'He couldn't have.'

'I think women mostly love more than men,' said Anne. 'Not always, but mostly.'

Lucy was silent, frowning.

'But he did love her,' said Anne, 'and that's why he talked about her – just as he talked about you. He didn't call you "Tigs" then. It was always "my darling little Lucy."'

Lucy's face closed in, and Anne felt that she had blundered.

'Oh, Lucy,' she said, 'I don't want to – to invade your most private life and memories but...'

'But you do want to marry my father,' said Lucy.

It was like a knockout blow in a sparring match. Anne found she had nothing more to say. She did want to marry Lucy's father, and if Lucy said no, that was the end of it. What use would arguments be?

Then, suddenly, Lucy gave in.

'All right,' she said. 'I don't mind. As you say, I shan't be living at home much longer, and if that's what he wants ... You can tell him that if he wants to marry you, I've no objection.'

Anne hesitated.

'Don't you think,' she suggested gently, 'that you might tell him yourself?'

Lucy was silent for a moment. Then she gave a shrug.

'All right,' she said.

Anne turned toward the hall, and Lucy followed her. Anne wanted to take her in her arms. 'Darling Lucy,' she could imagine herself saying, 'thank you. I love him. I'll do my best to make him happy. Thank you for understanding.' It was a charming idea, but it never became reality. Lucy opened the door, and Anne stepped outside and turned. Their eyes met for a second before Lucy closed the door and Anne heard the chain go on again.

Anne was in bed and nearly asleep when she heard the telephone ring. It was Tom's voice, excited and happy.

'Anne. Darling!'

'Tom?'

'It's all right,' he said. 'Lucy left a note on my pillow. I found it when I got in tonight. Such a sweet note.'

'Oh,' said Anne. 'What did it say?'

'I'll read it to you,' said Tom joyfully. 'Here it is. "Darling Daddy, sorry I was such an idiot. Anything you do is all right with me. Love, Lucy."'

'Lucy' thought Anne. Not 'Tigs'!

'Isn't that marvelous?' said Tom.

'Marvelous,' said Anne.

Nineteen

Anne asked Bender to give her away.

'You don't mean you really want them at the wedding?' demanded Tom in astonishment. 'That was a joke!'

'I know,' said Anne, 'but ... the Benders were there when we fell in love, and he was there when we parted. When you get married, someone is supposed to give you away from the old life to the new, and in a funny way Bender seems like the right person.'

Until she began making the arrangements for the wedding, she hadn't realized how complicated they were going to be.

'What with me marrying a widower and both my parents dead, I feel like suggesting that we should have the service in the churchyard at Endersby,' she remarked to Jean, who had agreed to be her maid of honor and had come to London to help her choose her wedding dress.

'The mauve would be very becoming to madam,' said the Marshall & Snelgrove assistant.

'Yes,' replied Anne, catching Jean's eye. 'Thank you, but I think I prefer the blue.'

'Well, what I say is,' agreed the *vendeuse*, a lady of advanced years whose hair was a very strange ginger, 'powder-blue always makes one look youthful. And with a nice feathered hat to go with it ... Shall I leave madam to try it on?'

'Yes. Thank you,' said Anne, and, when she had gone, added with an indignation that was only partly humorous, 'What did she mean, "makes one look youthful?" I know I've aged ten years in the last few months, but still ... Perhaps I'd better settle for the mauve after all.'

260

'Certainly not,' replied Jean. 'People will take you for the bridegroom's mother. They always tend toward the funereal.'

But when the powder-blue dress was on, Anne stood and looked at herself in the mirror in dismay.

'She's right,' she said. 'I look like Anna Neagle being girlish.'

'It's rather odd,' said Jean, 'not to be married in white, when after all...'

'I know,' answered Anne. 'But Tom in his widower's weeds and me all virginal white satin and net veil, it would look rather...'

'One drooping, one auspicious eye.'

'Yes,' said Anne. 'Lucy's going to droop as it is.'

She took of the powder-blue dress with its girlish ruffle, and stood looking at herself in her petticoat. She couldn't wear white, and she didn't want to look as if she had just gone out to 'buy an outfit' for the occasion, like the bride's mother and all the wedding guests. She wanted something personal, as the bridal gown always was.

'I shall wear primrose,' she said, suddenly. 'Very pale primrose, If I can't buy it here, I'll get Phyllis to have it made for me.'

'Good idea,' said Jean, but Anne caught a slight grimace.

'What's the matter?'

'It's just that if I wear primrose too, with my sallow complexion, I shall be yellow from head to foot. Everyone will think I've got jaundice.'

'No-o,' said Anne. 'You wear a lovely delicate violet.'

'Very clever!' exclaimed Jean, admiringly. 'I'm drooping, and you're auspicious.'

They grinned at each other.

'Now,' said Jean, 'all we have to do is to find two hats. Yours is no problem. A nice little primrose straw with a veil, but mine...! With a small face, thin hair, and no bosom, the only hat I can wear is a pillbox, and then I look like an escapee from the Boys' Brigade!'

Anne had never been more grateful for anything than she was now for the existence of the Newnham Family. They had had a grand reunion in London and took her out to dinner to celebrate the engagement. Freda was pursuing some obscure genetic research at the Cavendish, Jean was doing something brilliant in mathematics at Luton, and Sarah had married a doctor in Derby.

'What on earth happened to Derek?' demanded Anne, remembering Sarah's triumphant return from the Boat Race Ball with an engagement ring on her finger.

'Oh, wasn't it awful?' said Sarah. 'As soon as he stopped being in the Cambridge Boat, I discovered what an oaf he was, and I broke it off. He was furious.'

'Still,' said Freda, 'better then than later. I dare-say he wouldn't have been too pleased to discover that he had to put on a dirty vest and row up and down the river every night in order to revive matrimonial enthusiasm.'

They all giggled disgracefully, and Anne, giggling with them, reflected that it must have been quite distressing for Sarah at the time. That was why to this strangely assorted Family she could tell something of the truth of her forthcoming marriage – although, even to them, not the whole truth. She found it obscurely satisfying, too, that it was no betrayal to tell each other's secrets because the essence of a family is to know each other's secrets and to love each other in spite of everything so that pretense becomes pointless.

'Do you know Jean's thinking of marrying Dougal?' asked Freda, when Jean had gone to the ladies' room.

'*Dougal?* Is he still around? That frightful little Scotsman?'

'She said he's so frightful that if she marries him, she won't feel she's being disloyal to Graham,' explained Sarah. 'I mean, no

263

one could believe that she's given her heart to Dougal.'

'But that's dreadful,' said Anne.

'And she does want children,' said Freda.

'I know,' said Anne solemnly, 'but...'

Her solemnity suddenly gave way to irresponsible mirth.

'Goodness!' she said. 'Just think of all those little Dougals and Jeans trotting around the most expensive hotels in the world, leaving cheap tips.'

'The little Jeans will leave five pounds, just to compensate,' said Sarah. 'Everyone's going to get very confused.'

She and Freda laughed, and Anne laughed with them, but as Jean returned, Anne felt a certain melancholy creeping in. This was really the end of the Family. They would all be married except for Freda. She was becoming every year more severely academic, as though her parents had finally put Little Lord Fauntleroy to flight. Perhaps they would all continue to meet for lunch or dinner once a year, and then they would miss a year or two but still exchange Christmas cards. And then they would move and lose each other's addresses, until at last, like orphaned children, they would vanish into the great, wide world and never see each other again. But meanwhile, thought Anne, thank God they were all there to see her through the wedding!

The Family warmly applauded her determination to be married, as Freda put it, 'on neutral territory.' Tom had suggested having the reception at Wimbledon, and Pauli had offered to have Anne married from Twyford Cottage, but Anne didn't fancy either of these arrangements. To be married from the Wimbledon house, she felt, would be like holding the ceremony at Betty's graveside, and though Pauli's house would be better, Anne had a feeling that she would be swamped by Tom's family and friends and would become permanently known simply as 'Tom's second wife.' Besides, it was the custom for the bride's family to arrange the wedding and, as her family weren't around, Anne felt that it was up to her. She discussed it with Tom with a certain degree of honesty, but since the scene with Lucy, they had never quite recovered the marvellous openness that for a little while they had enjoyed. They could not help knowing that they were walking hand in hand through a minefield in which unspoken thoughts and secret emotions might now blow up in their faces.

It was Phyllis who unexpectedly provided the solution to the wedding arrangements.

'Why don't you settle for a nice hotel?' she suggested. 'The Regent Palace. They do these things very well. You can have the reception there, rent a room to change in – much easier all around.'

'A hotel!' cried Anne. 'What a good idea!'

Not perhaps, she thought, the Regent Palace – and the Grosvenor House would be much too expensive, but ... in the end, she found a hotel in South Kensington near the flat and booked a room for herself, another for the Benders, and one where Tom could leave his luggage and change after the reception. It meant that they could be married in the nearby church where she had worshipped since she came to London, so that seemed the next best thing to Endersby.

Tom came with her to interview the manager of the hotel, to see the rooms and to arrange the details of the reception, and together they went to see the vicar. They chose the hymns and the psalms and even the organ voluntary. But all the time Anne was thinking, 'There's something wrong. It'll never happen.'

For Tom, too, there was a feeling of unreality. It was partly because it was the second time he had been married, and, different as it was, it carried with it innumer-

266

able echoes. As he and Anne discussed the list of guests, he remembered Betty's mother saying, 'Oh, we must have Mr Blenkinsop. He gave Pauli a silver entrée dish. Solid silver!' Mention of champagne recalled his father: 'I hope they haven't bought the best; when it comes to champagne, nobody knows the difference.' One of the phrases Tom remembered using most frequently to Betty was, 'Do we really have to...?' Since Anne's conception of a quiet wedding was the same as his, he didn't have to use it this time. But after the children had gone back to school, Pauli came up to London to discuss the final details, and suddenly he found that he and Anne were saying at the same moment, 'Oh, do we really have to...?' and then looking at each other and laughing.

'Lucy will be bridesmaid, I suppose,' said Pauli.

'Oh, no!' exclaimed Tom quickly, and then tried to catch himself, and glanced at Anne.

'No, I don't think that's a good idea,' said Anne. 'I'm just going to have a maid of honor – an old Newnham friend.'

'Right,' said Pauli after a brief hesitation. 'Now, Tom, about the flowers...'

And suddenly Tom found himself back in a conversation about carnations and bouquets and remembered Betty saying, 'Get a corsage for Aunt Glad. She'd really appreciate that.' There were times when he felt that he was trying to marry Anne but kept getting caught up in memories of that earlier version of events. It was like taking part in a dream sequence in a Hollywood musical, where he danced in slow motion toward Anne in her bridal gown, and at the last moment the mist cleared and he was confronted not with Anne but with Betty or, more disconcertingly, with Lucy, holding her arms out to him and sobbing.

Tom had invited Bill Osmund and Peter Brent to the wedding with their wives, but he didn't have a stag night. Neither did he spend the evening with Anne. Jean was coming to stay the night at the flat, and she and Anne and Phyllis were going out to dinner together. Lucy and Colin had come home for their summer holidays the day before, and Tom spent a quiet evening at home with them. Too quiet, really, since they hardly mentioned the next day's events and certainly never spoke of how they felt about them.

Tom felt uneasy about being separated from Anne that evening, and he wondered if she felt the same. He could hardly have invaded her hen party, and yet it seemed wrong, somehow, for him to be alone with Lucy and Colin, as though they drew together into their little family citadel, leaving Anne on the outside.

When Tom went up to bed and looked in on the children, as Betty always used to and as he did now, Colin suddenly sat up in bed.

'Dad?'

Tom came to him quickly.

'Aren't you asleep?'

He heard a strangled noise.

'Dad, you won't forget Mum, will you?'

'No!' cried Tom. 'No, of course not!'

He put his arms around Colin and felt the stocky little body shaking against his and heard the great hoarse sobs and gulps of grief. He remembered Colin's stolid, expressionless face at Betty's funeral, and realized that this was the release of the sorrow that Colin had felt but never shown at his mother's death. And suddenly Tom, holding him close, was crying too, as he had not cried before, for the young, not very clever girl whom he had married and who had first experienced sex with him on her wedding night. She never took to it much, but because she loved him, she learned to give him pleasure, and she gave him also two beloved children. As he prepared to leave her for this second marriage, which he so

269

much desired, he felt he was truly mourning her for the first time.

Colin stopped crying and fell asleep in the same moment, like a small child. Tom laid him down, covered him over and, as he wiped his own tears away, found himself smiling. If only all griefs could be so swiftly and simply expressed! He opened Lucy's door. There was no sound. He went close to the bed. Through the window the moonlight shone on that small, delicate face, sleeping quietly. Tom stood for a long time looking down at her, wishing that she would wake, that they could talk, that he could be sure that all was well with her.

It was Anne's suggestion that they should all have lunch together at the hotel before the ceremony.

'You can't!' Pauli had protested. 'You and Tom mustn't see each other on your wedding day until you meet at the church.'

'Oh, nonsense!' said Anne. 'I'm sure to see Tom when he arrives at the hotel with his luggage – and you and David and Joan will have driven up from Hampshire – you've got to have lunch *somewhere*. Besides, we're going to be a family, so let's start off with a family lunch.'

'Well,' said Pauli, yielding, but still fighting

270

a rearguard action for the proprieties, 'I suppose we can have Squadron Leader Bender and his wife and your maid of honor, and call it a sort of wedding breakfast.'

And, uninvited and unwelcome, Anne found in her mind the words, 'The funeral bakemeats did coldly furnish forth the marriage table.'

'Well, well!' cried Bender cheerily over the *weinerschnitzel*, 'we never thought *this* would happen, eh?'

'*You* might not,' said Mavis, who was resplendent in emerald green and peacock-feathered hat and who had been drinking whiskey solidly ever since they arrived, 'but *I* did, the first time I ever saw 'em together.'

Tom and Anne exchanged a fleeting glance in which they silently agreed that they could have done without Mavis's prescence at this moment, reminding Lucy and anyone else who cared to note it that he and Anne had first loved each other while Betty was still alive.

Tom had forgotten how completely Mavis could paralyze all normal social intercourse, and he guessed that Anne had, too. Or perhaps it was just that this lunch party had not been such a good idea, anyway. Perhaps that was why these stupid rules were made about bride and groom not meeting on their

271

wedding morning – and perhaps they were not so stupid after all. Anne had a look of extreme weariness, as though she had been fighting a war for too long and had lost the will to win. When her eyes met his, it was with that dead, glazed look that people used to have after night duty, when they didn't care if the bombs fell, or where. They just wanted to sleep. He wished now that he could have seen Anne for the first time in the church, coming toward him up the aisle, radiant and full of confident love.

'Where are you going on your honeymoon?' asked Mavis. 'Or is it a secret?'

As Anne hesitated, Pauli intervened.

'It's a secret,' she said with a fixed smile. 'Not even David and I know.'

That was a complete lie, of course. Tom had always admired Pauli's gift for instantaneous and totally convincing lying. Tom would never have left the children without making sure that he could be reached in case of emergency. Since Tom's parents were in poor health, it had been agreed that they should not come to the wedding but that he and Anne should spend the first night of their honeymoon with them in Dorset and then go on to Cornwall. But a secret honeymoon destination was part of the wedding ritual, and even if it hadn't

272

been, Tom suspected that Pauli would not have confided it to Mavis, drunk or sober. Mavis turned unexpectedly to Colin.

'And what are you going to do,' she inquired, 'while your Daddy and your new Mummy are away? Are you and your sister going to stay and keep house together?'

'No,' replied Colin shortly. 'We're going to stay with Aunt Pauli.'

He obviously didn't like Mavis and didn't care who knew it.

'We always spend most of the summer there, anyway,' added Lucy.

'Yes,' said Pauli, smiling at her, 'we shall have to make the most of you this time. We shan't be seeing quite so much of you from now on.'

'Why not?' asked Lucy quickly.

'Well, old thing,' said David, in his bluff soldier manner, 'you'll be spending your holidays with your father and Anne, won't you?'

'Oh yes, of course,' said Lucy and smiled brightly.

To Tom that bright smile was like a stab to the heart. He knew in that instant that he had been trying to deceive himself and that the truth had been bound to come rushing back sooner or later. How could it be otherwise, when he knew Lucy so well and loved her so much? He knew, and had known all along, that Lucy hated the idea of him marrying again and that she was utterly miserable.

'It'll never work,' he thought. 'If it makes Lucy unhappy, we haven't got a chance.'

Jean and Pauli, talking cheerfully about holidays and travel abroad, had managed to silence Mavis for the moment, and Anne joined in occasionally, but she still had that glazed look in her eyes. Tom was horrified to find himself thinking that if he could, he would cancel the wedding in that moment. He could almost see himself standing up and saying, 'Anne – everyone – hang on a minute!' But what would he say after that?

'Anne, I can't marry you, because I love my daughter more than I love you'?

And, even if he said it, it wouldn't be true. What *was* true, though, Tom thought, was that their marriage could never survive the constant, accusing presence of Betty's daughter reminding them that their love began, like an adulterous child, when it had no right to exist. There could be no hope of a normal family life if every quarrel was going to form itself around well-worn battle standards – Tom and Lucy on one side and Anne, perhaps and fatally, with Colin's support, on the other.

If he could have been certain that Anne knew all this and was still prepared to take the chance, then Tom would gladly have done the same, just as the night-fighter pilots accepted the dangers and still flew. But he knew too well that she was not fitted for this kind of warfare and that it would destroy her as well as their marriage. He saw himself, Anne, Lucy, and Colin all together on a flimsy raft of love, plunging toward a destructive maelstrom, and there was nothing he could do to stop it.

The chilly remnants of the *weinerschnitzel* were taken away. Only Colin, Bender, Mavis, and David had conscientiously cleared their plates. The ice cream was brought, and conversation languished.

'Come on, Anne,' said Jean, with a cheeriness almost worthy of Bender, 'you ought to go and change. Mustn't keep them waiting at the church *too* long.'

As they stood up and the men stood up with them, there were a few moments of chatter about cars – who was going with whom, and at what time, and Tom's eyes met Anne's for a second in one anguished, panic-stricken glance. Then she was gone. As he sat down again, Lucy, from across the table, gave him another dazzling smile, like Ariel dying.

Being propelled up the stairs by Jean to dress for her wedding was like being back at Newnham and dressing for the May Ball. And Anne felt this even more when they found Freda and Sarah lurking outside her hotel bedroom.

'Come on!' said Freda. 'Don't be late. He might think better of it and say, "No"!'

They all laughed, and walked into the room where Anne's dress and hat were laid out on the bed.

'Where's Richard?' asked Anne.

'Taking Phyllis to the church,' answered Sarah, and added, 'Greater love hath no husband.'

Anne joined in the general giggle.

'Greater love hath no husband,' she said, 'than attending the wedding of his wife's girlfriend. How did you talk him into it?'

'*Talk him into it?*' repeated Sarah. 'I told him that if he didn't come, I'd tell his receptionist she was underpaid. What is marriage without blackmail? Anne, you have a lot to learn!'

Anne laughed with the others and thought that this was her last time of disgraceful irresponsibility.

'How was the lunch?' inquired Freda.

'Dire!' said Anne.

'I thought it might be. Men always have

276

second thoughts about marriage. The great thing is never to allow them to express them. Now, are you all set? Something old, something new, something borrowed, something blue.'

Anne was aware of secret glances and of a Family conspiracy, before Sarah produced a little box.

'Something new, anyway,' she said.

'From us,' said Freda.

'Good luck,' said Jean.

It was a tiny gold necklace with a minute diamond in a heart of gold.

'You can wear it under your dress,' said Jean.

'To celebrate the One that Nearly Got Away but didn't quite!' said Freda.

'Thank you,' said Anne, and kissed them.

It was the first time they had kissed, and they were all slightly embarrassed, as though they had never before admitted how much they had needed each other in those first, floundering days when the war was newly over.

'We'd better go,' said Freda. 'See you in church.'

'Yes,' said Anne. 'See you in church.'

'Come on, Anne,' said Jean, bustling about her as she sat at the dressing table. 'It's nearly time. I'll get your hat.'

Anne looked at herself solemnly in the mirror.

'I can see why brides wear veils,' she said. 'I look like death. I wish I had some rouge.'

'Better not,' said Jean. 'Get a bit hot and excited, and you'll turn puce in the face. That's not what they mean by 'the blushing bride!''

Anne tried to smile but couldn't. Jean turned away to fetch the hat, and in that instant everything that had been building up inside Anne for the past three months broke unexpectedly and irretrievably through, like a flood of water through a broken dam.

'I can't do it!' she said.

'What?'

Jean turned back, startled.

'I can't marry him.'

'Why on earth not?'

'Because of Lucy – and Betty.'

'Anne,' said Jean, as though she thought Anne had suddenly gone mad, 'Betty's dead. He's free.'

'No,' answered Anne, 'he'll never be quite free. Betty left him Lucy and Colin. They're still a family, and I can't break them up. It would make us all miserable. And besides – I did something awful.'

She saw Jean's face, fascinated, in the mirror.

'What did you do?'

'I went and saw Lucy,' said Anne, 'and bullied her into agreeing to the marriage.'

'Fine,' said Jean. 'Quite right, too!'

'Yes, but Tom didn't know.'

'So much the better,' said Jean. 'You won't tell him, will you?'

Anne looked up at her. Jean shrugged apologetically.

'Not very ethical, perhaps,' she said, 'but you've gotten away with it...'

'Have I?' said Anne. 'Can you imagine our first real quarrel – and Lucy involved in it, as she certainly would be? Tom says to Lucy, "You agreed to the marriage," and Lucy says, "Only because she *made* me!" And then it all comes out. Collapse of slender marriage.'

Jean put her hands on Anne's shoulders.

'Come on, Anne,' she said. 'Come on – chance it!'

They looked at each other in the mirror.

'I can't,' said Anne. 'If it was *my* husband and *my* daughter, I'd want to think that they still cared. If I marry Tom and it makes Lucy unhappy, I'll feel that what we did all those years ago was wasted.'

Jean took her hands away.

'Well, I do see,' she said helplessly, 'but – Anne, are you *sure*?'

279

'Quite sure,' answered Anne. 'Jean, you'll have to tell him.'

'Who, *me*?' cried Jean, healthily aghast.

'Please, Jean, quickly! Before he leaves for the church.'

'What shall I tell him?' Jean demanded.

'Just say I can't marry him, and ask him to take care of everything.'

'Anne, I'm sure you ought to tell him yourself.'

'No, I don't want to see him. It'll take too long and everyone will be waiting and ... and if he gets to the church and then I don't turn up, it'll be too awful. *Please*, Jean. Please, hurry!'

Jean went to the door and then turned with a despairing look.

'Anne, are you *sure*?'

'Quite sure,' said Anne.

When Jean had gone, she sat motionless, remembering Lucy's bright, anguished smile and the expression on Tom's face when he saw it.

It was all over, and she was glad. Ever since that awful evening when Lucy said, 'It's disgusting!' Anne had known in her heart that one of them must put an end to it, had known, too, that she had to be the one and was ashamed to have left it so late. Poor Tom, he felt the same as she did, but he could hardly jilt her on her wedding day.

'Thank heaven,' she thought, 'that I didn't buy a wedding dress. A proper twit I should look, sitting here in a white bridal gown, like Miss Haversham!'

She would rent that flat in Chelsea, she supposed. Occasionally Tom would come and take her out to dinner till, in the end, he became a sort of Old Dependable like Ted Brook, except that, now and again, she would remember that once they had loved each other. She remembered Phyllis saying, 'I'm not the marrying kind.'

'Perhaps I'm not either,' thought Anne.

She wondered what Tom would do when Jean told him. She knew that he would understand perfectly. They had never really tried to deceive each other, except for a little while in those foolish, primrose-picking days, but during the last few months, they had tried to deceive themselves, and that was what had made them both so uneasy. With Lucy feeling as she did and at such a vulnerable age, they couldn't get married now, and they both knew it. The sensible thing would be for Tom to go straight to the church and to apologize to the guests and to the vicar and call the whole thing off. And yet – she partly hoped and partly dreaded that he would come and argue the point

281

with her, however inevitable the outcome might be, and when the door opened, she turned quickly and knew that hope was stronger. But it was not Tom. It was Lucy.

'Hello,' said Lucy.

'Hello,' said Anne.

Lucy came in, leaving the door open. Anne stood up and turned to face her.

'It's me, isn't it?' said Lucy.

Anne was taken aback.

'Not altogether,' she said.

Lucy stopped short and looked her directly in the eye.

'You said you wouldn't let me beat you,' she said.

'I haven't,' said Anne. 'Not entirely. We'll just ... wait a year or two. You may feel differently then.'

'I shan't,' said Lucy.

'Oh,' said Anne, shaken.

Lucy stood with her feet together, very light and still in her leaf-green, full-skirted suit, a Juliet-cap on her fine, fair hair.

'I shan't ever want you to marry Daddy,' she said. 'It's no good saying I would. When Mummy died – it was horrible, but – but I thought, at least now I'll have Daddy to myself.'

Somewhere at the back of her mind, Anne knew that it was immensely important that

282

Lucy should make such an intimate and vulnerable confidence to her, but she was too tired to register it.

'You don't think,' she suggested, with a note of despair rather than hope, 'that we might share him?'

Lucy scowled.

'It wouldn't be easy.'

'Oh, God!' said Anne, turning away, and her voice broke from sheer exhaustion, 'nothing's easy!'

She became aware of Lucy flying toward her across the room and turned quickly, almost thinking that Lucy was going to hit her, but instead Lucy clasped her around the waist in a fierce, silent embrace.

'Oh, Tigs!' said Anne, and then catching herself up, 'I'm sorry – I didn't mean to call you...'

Lucy looked up at her between tears and laughter.

'If you're going to marry my father,' she said, 'I think you'd better call me "Tigs"!'

Then Jean was in the doorway saying, 'Is it on or off?'

'It's on!' cried Lucy, and suddenly it was all a game, an adventure to her.

She kissed Anne and darted to the door and turned, her green eyes dancing.

'I told Dad to go on to the church with

283

Uncle David. And all the others were going on as well except for Aunt Pauli and Colin – they're waiting for me – and Squadron Leader Bender, of course.' She paused. 'He's had rather a lot of snifters,' she remarked.

'Never mind,' said Anne. 'If I can just get him to the church, Mavis will take over.'

'She's had quite a lot of snifters, too!' said Lucy.

Anne suddenly realized that the Bender joke was no longer hers and Tom's but Lucy's as well, and she felt a tiny pang of loss. Nothing is for nothing in this world.

'Here's your hat,' said Jean, straightening the crumpled veil.

'Don't be long!' Lucy adjured from the doorway.

'Lucy!' called Anne.

Lucy turned, poised for flight, a bright, inquiring look on her face.

'How did you...? I mean, what did you tell your father?'

The brilliant, triumphant smile was like a flash of lightning.

'I told him not to worry, I'd fix it!' said Lucy, and vanished.

Anne took the hat from Jean, and their eyes met.

'You've got a right one there!' said Jean.

284

'Don't I know it!' Anne replied. 'Oh, well, hope for the best,' and she put the primrose straw hat firmly on her head.

Tom, sitting beside David in the front pew, looked over his shoulder and saw Lucy and Pauli come in with Colin. Lucy gave him a dazzling smile, and Pauli a grimace that said, 'Let's hope everything's all right now!' Colin's face was grimly expressionless as though, totally confused, he hoped to survive by giving nothing away. Tom saw Freda and Sarah and Mavis Bender engaged in a sort of seated jig as they shuffled down the pew to make an empty space for Bender and then shuffled back as Phyllis and Richard decided to move into the next pew so that Sarah could sit with her husband. Out of the corner of his eye, Tom caught a glimpse of Bill Osmund – now divorced from the East End wife of his bosom – sitting with his bored-looking, smart-as-paint new model. Beyond them, Peter and Eileen Brent glanced at each other and then toward the door at the back of the church.

There were too many people around, thought Tom, just as there always had been, except for a few brief idyllic moments. He remembered parting in The Reed Thatcher in 1944, and had the frightening, irrational

285

that when Anne finally came up the
and took his hand, they would look at
other and say, 'Good-bye, darling.'
ood-bye.'

The organ music changed, and there was
a scuffle as the congregation got to its feet.
David nudged Tom, and he stood up and
turned. He saw Anne in her simple prim-
rose-coloured dress and the little straw hat
with a veil. He knew afterward that there
had been other people there – Bender,
somewhat rubicund; Jean, anxious in pale
violet; and the vicar – but he didn't see
them. He only saw Anne, coming toward
him, happy and radiant, full of confident
love. Her eyes met his and they smiled at
each other, and nobody else existed, nothing else mattered.